WHAT BECAME OF THEM
& OTHER STORIES FROM
FRANCO-AMERICA

WHAT BECAME *of* THEM

and other stories from
FRANCOAMERICA

by Denis Ledoux

[S☀P] SOLEIL PRESS [⚜⚜]

Designer: Martha Blowen

Soleil Press
   RFD#1, Box 452
   Lisbon Falls, Maine 04252

Printed in the USA

Publisher's Cataloging in Publication Data
Ledoux, Denis, 1947-
  What Became of Them and Other Stories From Franco-
  America.
    CONTENTS: Germaine.-- What Became of Them.--
  Desneiges.   (etc.)
    1. Short Stories, Franco-American -- Maine. 2. Maine --
      fiction.
    I. Title.
    L.C. Number 87-062312
    ISBN 0-9619373-0-0

Stories in this book first appeared in full or in part in the following publications:
    Puckerbrush Review--*Dinora, Germaine*
    New Maine Writings II--*What Became of Them*
    Le Canado--*Dinora, Desneiges*
    Le FAROG Littéraire--*What Became of Them*
    Kennebec XII--*Looking Back*

for Martha

femme de mes rêves

femme de mes jours

I want to express my thanks to Martha Blowen for her indefatigable help and support over the years it has taken to write these stories and over the months it has taken to ready them for publication, to my children Zoë and Maxim for their cooperation and patience while "Papa is working on his book", to my friend and fellow writer Michael Murphy for his many hours of invaluable technical assistance and for the use of his word processing system.

Contents

The characters in these stories are fictional. They are not representations of real people in the past or the present. Most of them are composites of people I have known: I have borrowed the features of one, the hopes and disappointments of another. As a writer, I have invented much from the inspiration of the people I love.

PART I

Germaine

"It'll be all right. We'll make out," Thomas said. He reached across the wagon seat to pat Germaine's hands which she held tightly in the folds on her lap.

Across the gravel road, *le rang St-Ignace,* Monsieur Boucher's Holsteins, there were about twenty of them, continued to graze toward the stream. The big black one, *la grosse noire,* led as usual; her udder, empty now, would bulge and scrape against the rocks later when, at the end of the day, she led the herd back to the barn.

Milking time! Where would they be then? On the road someplace! All of it was very strange: she had never been more than twenty miles from the village. Later, in Maine, many years later, whenever she saw a black cow, she thought of *la grosse noire.* What had become of her? she wondered in the same way she sometimes wondered what had become of Mme Deshêtres or of Mme Boucher.

"We'll make out all right," repeated Thomas. He gave Reine, the draft horse they were to leave at his brother's in the village, a gentle tug. Reine walked towards the road and turned south. Slowly, she began to pull the heavily-loaded wagon towards the village. St. Jude lay nine miles to the south and many hundred feet below.

"Oh, I know," she said, turning to look at him. "I'm being

foolish, but I can't help saying what I feel. I wish there were some means, some way, we could try for one more year."

To the right, across the valley, perched high on a range of hills, the silver-painted roof of the church at Ste-Hélène de Beresford shone brightly. How many times had she seen this roof shine in the morning -- summer and winter -- when she had walked from the barn to the kitchen to get breakfast for the children!

When he had locked the door this morning, she had said she was being locked out of her life. It wasn't fair to him, she knew, to say that. It had hurt him that morning as much as it had hurt her to walk around the empty house.

They crossed the stream. The water was low. For the second year, there had been too little rain during the summer and too little snow during the winter.

"No more lugging water," he said.

But that moment, she would have gladly hauled water all year long. Two years ago, the pipe leading to the kitchen pump had frozen in March. This was before Dinora was born. They had had to lug water from the stream. The water did not flow in the pipe until the beginning of June. Many times, as she carried water to wash diapers, she had wished herself elsewhere. If only she could undo that wishing now!

After a straight course, where the road began to climb between a double row of maples, they passed the schoolhouse. She turned to look at her children. There were four of them then: Marin, Florianne, Ilda, and Dinora. Lately, the older ones had begun to talk of the large schoolhouse they would attend, of the new friends they would make. But, neither they nor she had any idea what it would be like in the States. She did not know much about schoolwork; she knew about other things, about gardening and herbs and sewing. She regretted not knowing more about schoolwork but there hadn't been the time for that. There had been time for the farm.

She sighed. How were they going to survive in a place where what they knew wasn't what you had to know?

"Germaine, we have to go."

"Yes, I know."

Jean Thibeau, the man who had wanted to marry her but whom she had refused for Thomas, had become a prosperous farmer. He had received money from his father and had started in a big way. She would not be going if she had chosen differenly. But, the very thought embarrassed her: it was disloyal to Thomas. She loved Thomas. It was only that the day, this day, was so difficult.

In the city, they would live in a tall building with many other people. The children would go to a large school. She herself would work in a factory with Thomas, but she didn't know how much of this would be good for the children, good for Thomas and herself.

"Stop. Stop," she shouted to Thomas.

He looked at her.

"It's Mademoiselle Lizotte!"

A young woman, dressed in a simple blue wool dress that swept against the sill, appeared at the doorway of the school. The building had been painted yellow when Germaine was a child at the school and, when she looked carefully, she could still see some yellow.

From the doorway, Mademoiselle waved and then she ran towards them. She had the strong body of a Canadian farm girl.

"We'll miss you," she said. Already she had lost three families in one year. "The children were asking after you kids. You be good children and show these American kids how much we can learn in a Canadian school. I know you can do it when you want to.'

"*Oui,* Mademoiselle," they answered from the rear of the wagon. She was still their teacher, somehow, as long as they were in Canada.

They had been good neighbors. The *rang* would seem empty without them, said Mademoiselle.

Germaine began to cry. "Oh, Mademoiselle, if only you knew how much I hate being in my shoes. We tried everything."

"I know you did. Perhaps you'll see your way to coming

back -- or perhaps you'll like it so much you won't want to
come back." Mademoiselle tried to smile.

They were quiet. Germaine looked up. Above, on the
school's weathervane, there perched a cardinal. It too had
stayed too long. They all three watched as it flew across the
field. Then it was gone. It would not come back.

They looked away from one another, knowing that people
too did not come back. One thing led to another: the children
grew older and married and did not want to return; the
money was too good or not good enough, and so they would
not be coming back.

"We'll miss you," she repeated simply.

Thomas answered, "We have cousins who will help us.
Perhaps we will like it so much we won't want to come back."

"You will be *un rich américain*," Mademoiselle laughed,
forgetting for a moment the import of what they were doing.
"You won't want to talk to us simple *canadiens*."

"Oh, *non*, we will never forget our home. *Jamais!*" Having
said this, Germaine looked down.

A silence fell on the group. Then Mademoiselle said, "No, of
course you won't forget. I must go back. The children are
waiting for their lessons."

The windows were filled with children waving. Mademoiselle
turned and walked down the weedy path and disappeared into
the building.

"*Envoie*, Reine. Let's get a move on."

Slowly, Reine plodded up the long dirt incline. The fields
were still green but soon the frosts and the cold would come.

"Oh, Mademoiselle," she had cried out, forgetting that
Thomas had said the more they talked about it, the more
painful the leaving would be. "And we will miss you,"
Mademoiselle had answered.

To the right, closed, the porch beginning to sag, one of the
dormers needing a window replaced, the Martineau house, the
house where as a young girl she had attended many *soirées*,
foretold what would become of their house. One day, they
would come back to visit and their porch would have caved in.

Some of the roof shingles might have come off and water have seeped inside, to warp the wooden walls and to pull the ceiling plaster down.

She and Thomas should have rented their house, of course. The Martineaus had wanted to rent their farm too but it was impossible. Everyone was trying to get out. There were empty places all around them.

Her hands which she still held tightly in her lap were strong hands. They had not only baked and washed but shovelled and planted and milked. They had done everything. There was nothing these hands could now do that would change things.

There was no money left to continue. Thomas had sold the harvest that otherwise would have gone into the root cellar. This sale had saved them from debt and had provided cash for the trip. It would be different in the States because they would work in a mill. Every week they would receive a pay check -- whether there was a cold snap or not, whether there was rainfall or not.

Oh, yes, she was being foolish. She knew it was the right thing to do. Thomas had tried his best. She had too. And the children. But, it had simply not been enough. Perhaps they could make a pile of money in the States and get on top of things and come back.

When she remembered that morning later on, as she sat in her kitchen by the big American oil stove, looking out over the roof tops to the mill where she had spent her days for more years than she was old the year they left, she remembered it was at that point that she had broken down into abandonned crying, in front of the Martineau house, because the porch was sagging.

Reine continued to plod up the hill. When they passed the Deshêtres place, a dog barked at them, a new dog she had never seen, hardly more than a puppy. Already things were changing.

Soon, too soon, they reached the crest of the hill. If she turned around she would be able to see their house. On many cold Sundays as she returned from the village, the sight of the house from there had warmed her.

Quickly, she turned.

"Look, children. *La maison.*"

They too turned to look at the house. It was painted blue with a white trim. Around two of the sides, the south and the west, ran a porch. Above the porch were two dormers. The children had slept upstairs. In back was the barn, a large wooden structure with a cupola. Behind were the orchards and the gardens and the pastures.

Soon they could see only the second floor; that disappeared, leaving only the top of the barn. Then the cupola too disappeared.

There was nothing left.

Wh at Becam e of Th em

He was like a rainstorm at harvest time.

What was she to do? She was a woman with children, a woman of certain years. She could not break into a rage -- it was not like her -- and she could not let him go unchallenged. He was ruining everything they had struggled to put together.

Before, in the evenings, when Florianne had watched Amédée through the gossamer curtains of her darkened front windows, she had thought when he went to the left that he was going to the Alouette Club. But, when he went to the right, walking beneath the red and yellow trees of early October, she supposed he was going to the Champlain.

Sometimes, after watching Amédée leave, she tarried in her front rooms. There were two rooms whose hardwood floors she had covered with "Persian" carpets. The walls were papered. The furniture in the room was recently reupholstered. Amédée called it her little *château;* she wanted to believe he was proud of what they had amassed. They had started with nothing and had created a well-furnished home for themselves, a place that was *comme il faut*. They had more than their parents. Their parents had had nothing but the farms and painful memories of having left them. Papa had said he and Maman were born to eat "a little bread". Her eyes fell on the

bright afghan she was sitting on. Her sister Ilda who was poor
had said it was beautiful and, to please her sister, Florianne
had offered to do one for her once Christmas was over. After
Christmas, too, after she had gone in enough as a spare hand
at the mill, she would buy a new radio, something with an
attractive console, something with dark wood.

She would sit quietly in her beautifully-appointed
livingroom, feeling contented with what she had put together,
but the children would begin to tussle in the kitchen and
scream, "Maman, tell her this," and "Maman, tell him that."
Nothing ever stayed the same. She would get up and return to
her duty in the brightly-lit kitchen. She was a woman; she
could not leave at night and relax in the society of her
friends. Her only company was the children who ran and
banged doors and screamed and scratched furniture. They were
as strident as the looms at the mill, she thought, but she
knew that that would change someday. Someday, they would
be grown up and she and Amédée would be alone again.

All of this was in 1934. That was the year Maman took sick.
She had been a strong woman. On the farm, she had helped
with the harvests; in the city, she had worked in one of the
mills until she retired. Before this year, Maman had always
canned a winter's supply of vegetables and fruits. And then, it
was age, she took sick. Taking one of the younger children to
prevent their fighting and tearing the house apart, Florianne
would spend evenings with Maman who was not sick enough
yet to leave her place. Maman did many things for herself,
but she found it difficult to keep the bathroom floor clean, to
lift the wet laundry out of the washing machine, to change
her bed.

The girls took turns to do this for Maman. Sometimes too
they brought soups; other times, bread. When Florianne could
not come on her scheduled night because she had been called
in as a spare hand on the second shift, Dinora or Ilda showed
up in her stead to talk with Maman and perhaps to darn a
used stocking. Now that it was getting colder, they talked of
doing a fall cleaning, a *grand ménage*.

Maman kept saying Canadians were too clean and they'd answer, "You're the one who made us this way." And Maman would laugh: she had very good girls. They may have been born to eat "a little bread" but they were happy together. She was more happy than sad and she knew that Papa would approve.

Maman lived in a four-room apartment on Horton Street. From her rocker in the green kitchen, she saw the sun rise. Every morning, she saw it rise as she had seen it rise since she was a little girl on the farm overlooking the Chaudière River. At night, because of the angle of her building, she did not see it set. When she had felt well, she had sometimes walked outside, to a spot down the street where the sun could be seen slipping into the horizon.

Almost every evening now, Amédée said that he thought he would take a walk down to the Champlain or, if it had been the Champlain recently, to the Alouette. Florianne might say, "Can't you stay here tonight, and watch the kids while I go to Maman's?" He would answer, "I'm too tired. Not tonight." She would not say anything because his foreman job entailed many exhausting responsibilities and she acknowledged that he needed to relax. It was his salary, after all, that had made the difference in her life, had made that she was not poor like Ilda.

Sometimes, she sat alone in the front rooms, after the younger children had been put to bed and Laurier, who was a good boy, and Muriel were up studying in the kitchen. The house was quiet like the street after the second shift at the mill when she walked home alone. At these times, Florianne could hear Papa's voice saying, "My girls would be better alone than with men who drink. Never trust a man who drinks." After all these years, she could still hear his voice from all the other voices in her memory just as once she had been able to pick out his voice from all the other voices at family parties, at the Christmas *réveillon* when everyone got together at the little apartment on Horton Street.

Papa would not be pleased with Amédée's going so often to

the Alouette or to the Champlain. When they had married, Amédée had never gone out. Now he was gone often; but, he never came back drunk. Sometimes, he did not even smell beer. Ilda's husband had always smelled beer. Florianne had never trusted him.

When it was exactly that Florianne had begun to uncover the presence of the other woman, whose name was Lise but whom Florianne was never able to dignify with a name, to make into a person, she was not sure. It had come initially as a result of jealousy: he was free to do anything. Although it sounded silly to her when she began, she decided to keep a watch on his salary. This was not easy since he got paid in cash and not by check. She felt justified, however, when it turned out that he did not know that Jos. Beaulieu, who was an *habitué* of the Alouette, had bought a new car. At the Champlain, Dinora's nephew-in-law had begun to wait on tables, but Amédée didn't seem to know that either. Little by little, in fact, it was fairly easy once she set her mind to it, Florianne discovered the other woman, a widow from Montréal, who lived in Ilda's parish.

"*Monstre, cochon,*" she shouted.

"Florianne, we aren't children anymore. We know these things happen." And to him that was enough, but Florianne felt foolish and threatened. She had worked for years to get what she had now. In some way, she would have to punish Amédée and keep together what they had assembled. She would not be an object of pity, a subject of gossip. And she would not be poor like Ilda -- not for another woman's benefit. She would not let go of her right to share in Amédée's foreman's salary. Amédée said he did not want to leave. He too was afraid. He was good to her for a while, but she would not let him come near her. She had seen too many bosses mollifying an employee for a dirty job to be fooled by Amédée. She told him he could stay for the children's sake, but he must never go out and do anything like that again. At that time, Laurier was sixteen and Muriel was twelve, and there were the other children who screamed and fought and broke things in her beautiful front rooms.

Then, Maman, who grew more sick, moved in at Marin's house. There was no room at Ilda's place. The year that Maman died, Ilda was living with her Rita on Oxford Street. They had a three-room apartment in Thibeau's block. It was the same apartment to which Ilda had moved after her husband and the boys had died. Before, on Shawmut Street, she had had double livingrooms with hardwood floors and sun all day long. But her husband had been a difficult man, she'd readily say, and they had taken to quarrel. They were like two barn fowls pecking at each other. While he was away at the mill, she would take the kids to Papa's on Horton Street. Late in the evening after he had finished his stint on the second shift, Ilda's husband would come pounding on Papa's door. Papa always stayed up on those nights and he always spoke to the two of them. Things could not go on like this, he'd say each time.

Then influenza came to the city. It decimated the population. In the end, Ilda lost her husband and the boys. The death of the boys affected her terribly. Something in her, she said, died with them. That was in 1918 and so that year she moved from the sunny apartment on Shawmut Street to Oxford Street where her windows opened up on an alleyway. Maman took care of little Rita while Ilda went to work in the mill down the ugly street.

Bates Street, where Florianne lived, still had trees, tall, thin elms which opened up prodigiously at the crown. Because of Amédée's foreman job, Florianne had a second floor apartment with eight rooms and a bath. The front rooms, the double parlors as they were called, opened up to the street. Through the triple windows, at that time of year, Florianne could see the street growing dark, leaves piled up on the sidewalk. She sat alone remembering the dingy rooms they had had in Canada and the dingy rooms Maman and Ilda had had all their lives. Florianne knew that she had been a lucky woman in many ways and that she would never give up any of what she had.

In the back of Florianne's apartment, off the kitchen, a large bedroom opened up to a yard with trees and swings. It was perfect for a sick person. The room was close to the bathroom, it had afternoon sun, it was fairly well sheltered from the street noise. It should have been Maman's room -- except for that pig Amédéc who slept there now. He had made life impossible in the apartment with his carousing. He and Florianne had begun to fight like cat and dog. Maman needed quiet. And so when finally Maman left her place for good, it was to Marin's apartment, at the corner of Oak and Sabattus, on the second floor back, that she went to. There, a small, dark room with dirty wallpaper had been prepared for her. Liane and Marin never fixed things up because their lives were dedicated to saving money. They were trying to get back to Canada.

The time came when Maman began to toss and turn all her nights, and Liane and Marin couldn't take care of her alone anymore. The sisters came to spend the nights with her, the three from Lewiston, and Albertine who made it up sometimes from Litchfield where she had a farm. Amédée, who really was fond of Maman, who had known her since he was an adolescent living in the block across the street, also spent nights with her now that he no longer went out carousing.

(Maman said to Florianne, "Take him back into your heart." Florianne could not, although she said she would. Amédée was not half the man Papa had been, she thought, Papa would be sad to see how things had changed.) It was Florianne who spent the last night with Maman. That night, after walking back from a second-shift stint at the Bates Mill -- Florianne was in the spinning room, the hot, stuffy spinning room that she didn't mind terribly because it was cold outside now and she was going to get herself new bedspreads with her income -- Florianne sat at the kitchen table crocheting doilies for her bedroom bureaus. She could hear Maman babble in the little room off the kitchen about inchoate things, about Canada, about the farm at St. Philippe.

"Thomas, Thomas, get the girls in, get the girls in," she

moaned. "There is a fox on the prowl. The Bonneau boys told
me they saw a rabid fox. Quick, Thomas."

"It's all right, Maman," said Florianne, going into the
bedroom to check on her mother. "There's no fox. We're in
Lewiston now. We're in the United States."

"No fox? Lewiston? What will the good father say when he
comes for his parish visit?"

When Florianne and the others had been little in Canada,
they had sat at night on the porch, rocking, and listening to
the crickets. The Bonneau children might come over and
sometimes the Dionne kids too. Papa talked about things in
the past --the hunts and the clearing of the fields, about his
parents and grandparents, and about the coming of the English
and about *les sauvages* before that. Life was different in those
days, he'd say. The Bonneau boys sometimes talked about their
uncle who worked in a textile mill in Lewiston. This uncle
who had a piano in his livingroom wanted them to come down
to *les Etats*. Their father, however, always said he preferred
holding on to what he already had.

"I never thought we would traipse around like this," Papa
had said, sitting in the apartment on Horton Street years
later. "I just meant to come earn my jackpot and then return
home. What are we doing here? Our people will dry up like an
old apple forgotten in a root cellar. We must stay together as
a family; we must stay together as *canadiens*." He was buried
alongside his own mother and father in the land of his
ancestors and, unless some miracle happened, Maman would
be buried in the USA. They were not staying together.
Everything was changing. They were leaving people behind
here and there. Movement was in their blood. They were
descendants of the *coureurs de bois* and the *voyageurs*. And
now Marin wanted to leave. He was saying, after Maman died,
he would go to Canada.

She thought, Would her life now melt away like snow in the
spring?

"But we will be at the mercy of the English in the USA. We
can't go. Don't worry, my darling, the harvest will be good

here," Maman muttered. So many times the harvest had not been good, Florianne remembered as dawn began to spread across the night like a bright new coverlet over a bed. She had lace curtains and new doilies and a full set of bedroom furniture on her mind.

"Let Marin go back and starve if he wants!" she said to herself, but she wanted him to stay. He was her brother.

On that morning, while Ilda was working the third shift at the Bates weaving room, the looms banging and clanging around her, Germaine Comtois, her mother, began her final passage into death. They called the mill. The foreman, who was a cousin of Amédée's, said he would let Ilda go right away. Laurier took his bicycle over to his aunt Dinora's house. A short while before, Marin would have telephoned the Biziers downstairs. They knocked twice on the pipes for Dinora to come down for a message, but the Biziers had moved out and the new people did not have a telephone.

They called Albertine in Litchfield. Her husband was gone to Vermont with the truck and so Mr. Desruisseaux, the retiree who lived across the hall from Marin, went out to get her at the farm. Litchfield was twenty miles away and so they did not get back until seven. The priest came, a Canadian peasant with a ruddy face and large hands, and administered Extreme-Unction as Laurier, who was sixteen and who was going to be a priest too, watched attentively. *Le bon père* anointed Maman's forehead, her eyes, her nose, her lips, her hands, and her feet with the holy oils, imploring God to grant Maman forgiveness for sins committed through the agency of her weak flesh.

At eleven that morning, in the dark little bedroom, surrounded by her girls, Florianne, Ilda, Dinora, Albertine, Desneiges and by her sons, Marin and Gédéon, Germaine Comtois died.

She was seventy-four.

In the afternoon, Marin called relatives in St. Philippe and Sherbrooke and Fall River. Because he was ashamed of his shabby apartment, the wake was at Florianne's. She began to rearrange her front parlor for the placing of the casket. The men rolled the piano out to the hallway. Neighbors brought food in. *Tortières, cretons, bouillies,* cold meats, pastries, cookies. Florianne cleaned out the back bedroom that should have been Maman's. Aunt Zélire and Uncle Georges from Fall River would be sleeping there in the room that overlooked the lovely back yard. They always stayed with her and Amédée whenever they came up. Amédée would sleep with Florianne that night but he must not try to touch her.

Toward suppertime, the casket was brought in. The dead then were kept in airtight caskets, under glass. Below the glass, Maman was at peace, wearing the soft pink dress the girls had bought her the summer before, her hair carefully arranged around her face. Although it was an unfamiliar hairstyle created by morticians, Florianne did not mind. It was not unbecoming to Maman. Florianne did not go to the mill that night where she had worked in the various rooms as a spare hand for years, living off Amédée's salary and using hers to acquire her things. Instead she sat in the big *fauteuil* and thought of Maman and cried.

Florianne was so alone. How would she cease to be a field dying of drought?

"Shame about Thomas being up there and her down here!"

"But there was no keeping him back. He said he was as strong as a bull. How are you going to tell someone like that that he can't go to his own brother's funeral? And now they're not together."

Later Florianne got up and helped the younger girls with the midnight meal and cried some more. She remembered the novenas Maman used to say for Laurier's vocation. She had wanted a priest in the family. Florianne would see to it that Laurier became a priest -- for Maman she would tend his vocation as one tends a kitchen garden. Already she was putting money away for his education.

Madame Lessard upstairs and Madame Masson downstairs had little children sleeping on their couches and beds. One by one, after the meal, the parents began to reclaim the sleeping

children and return to the relatives with whom they were
staying.

The wake lasted another day and then the next day, the day
of the funeral, before the body was brought to St. Pierre and
St. Paul's for the High Mass for the Dead, all the family was
to file through Florianne's parlor one final time.

"Fortunately, we aren't cramped at Marin's," Florianne said
to herself when she woke during the night, feeling the
unaccustomed weight of Amédée next to her. Her mother and
father had slept together all the days of their married life.

During that night, Madame Comtois' eyes and mouth,
propelled by inner pressures, opened wide. Her face pushed
against the transparent cover and her tongue flattened out on
the glass.

Forty years later, Muriel who had been twelve, could still
see her mémère with the monster face pushing against the
glass, her tongue flattened. That was a terrible memory which
Florianne was never able to forgive. She always associated it
with Amédée who had slept next to her that night. Later,
after the interment, Marin said that he would return to
Canada now that Maman was dead. Amédée called him a fool.
Marin however said, "So you think that repairing broken looms
and supervising spinning lots is a fit job for an *habitant!*"

"Maman always loved the farm," said Dinora, "but I could
never go back."

"Papa, too," said Desneiges.

"I'm going to find me a place. The thought of heading north
again has kept me going all this time. Hey, what kind of life
is it to work all day in dark, noisy rooms -- or all night for
that matter? It's not healthy. What's it getting you? I'm not
going to die in those brick caskets."

"We were born for misery," said Dinora. "We *canadiens* are
born for a little bread."

Florianne thought, "Now that Papa and Marin will both be
gone, I will be alone without a man." But she knew it would
not be the same as for Ilda.

"Nope, there's a farm for me back home with soil that isn't

too rocky. I'll need a woodlot that holds enough fuel to last many winters and a farmhouse and barns that are in good repair. With a herd of cows and a large garden, I'll be my own man. If I buy right, there'll be a maple grove with a lot of good years left to it. And you, you will be working for an hourly wage. That's what killed Papa."

"You're going to starve," said Florianne, envying his courage. She herself was afraid. When she thought of living on a farm again, she felt like a child before a snarling animal. She felt like a child asked to do an impossible task. She did not want to reacquaint herself with threadbareness.

Ilda said to Florianne that she would love to go back, that it would make her feel like a bird in spring to live in Canada again, but without a man it was impossible and men were too much of a bother.

Yes, I would go too, if I had a husband, thought Desneiges, but she said nothing to the others. She had never had a husband.

"Life is always tearing us apart," said Dinora, thinking of her own husband who wanted to leave the city to live in the country. "There is too much change. Papa would not be happy."

After Marin left, Amédée had, at first, tried to be friends with Florianne, but she had not let him. In later years, when they sat in different rooms, each beautifully appointed by Florianne, always spending their time alone, Amédée would wonder how his people had made such a woman. She was as hard as the maples which had grown around the villages in Canada. He said to himself that she was molded of the winter cold.

DESNEIGES

"*Mais, c'est impossible!*" she said.

There was no extra pie, but there were extra mashed potatoes.

The man grimaced and pulled his head from the service cubicle. As soon as his head was clear, Desneiges brought the panel down and locked it. She felt protected now, but she was so tired she wanted to cry. She poured herself a cup of coffee. From the poor house dining room came the man's muffled curses.

Twenty-eight and her future promised more years in the poor house kitchen, more years taking care of her brother Gédéon's children. And Blanche was pregnant again! For one more, Desneiges would be the old maid aunt, *ma tante la vieille fille,* sharing a room with a niece. And how soon would it be before there were two nieces in her room? Oh, where was the man with whom she could get away from all of this? And where were the children who would come from them, for whom she had hungered all this while?

The coffee gone too soon, she got up and continued with the cleaning. One more meal and there would be no cooking, for a week. If only her vacation in Montréal could stretch forever. To have no more meals at the poor-farm where the old ladies said she burned everything and the men wanted

more pie and swore at her! And she had no budget for
anything sufficient. Always trying to make miracles out of
what they brought in to her from the gardens or what people
donated. You never knew ahead of time what to expect.

And after all of this, home to Blanche and Gédéon and their
children. *Mon Dieu!* but she hadn't thought life would be this
way.

Desneiges, *la vieille fille!*

*

On her only foray into the center of Montréal, Desneiges
had been overcome by its size and so she had stayed the rest
of the week on Panet Street with Blanche's sister Anaïs.
Anaïs had four children and she sewed for English ladies in
Westmount. On the third evening of Desneiges' visit, Anaïs
held a *veillée* for her brother-in-law Gédéon's sister, a small
soirée with pastries and beer.

She was surrounded by good people who smiled and called
her *l'américaine.*

"Three years in Lowell were enough for me," said Edgar
whom she had just met. "The factories, the schedules, the
crowded apartments! Not a place for an *habitant,* for a man
from the farm."

And she looked at his hands, big-fingered hands with square
nails and, on the inside, earth stains on the ridges and prints,
like a tatoo.

The next evening, they walked to *le parc Lafontaine,* not
far from Anaïs's apartment and watched the ducks. There he
told her about his *concession,* the holding that he had
received from the government, up north, in Abitibi, how it
would be his someday and how he would have ducks. And
about the long winters that a man spent in the woods.

When he spoke, his eyes glistened and she felt his
excitement and envied his future. It would be his someday, if
he worked hard and long. Something would come of it for him
and for his children. When he had a woman. Someday. It was

that way for the settler. The *colon* who had a woman.

But she was going back on Saturday. She would take the train to Vermont, to White River Junction, before transferring to Lewiston. On Monday, she would be in the poor-house kitchen again, cooking for the residents who said she couldn't cook well and who wanted pie all the time and swore at her.

And at night, she would share a room with her neice. How soon would it be before there were two nieces with her? And she would be *ma tante la vieille fille* without a man, ever, for her in Lewiston.

Edgar was not young. He had once been an Oblate lay brother. Now he was alone. He needed a woman but what did he have to offer a woman?

He was a good, gentle man, she thought. That was a lot to offer a woman. It was something she would look for in the father of her children.

*

The land where their *concession* was was flat and the trees were short. In winter, daylight was brief and the air was very cold.

Every year after they were married, Edgar was away from November to April, in the woods, contracting his time for the money they needed to keep going.

The year she was forty-one, it was exceptionally cold and the snow blew steadily. By three in the afternoon, it was dark and she was afraid now. She was big with another pregnancy.

There had been five other times when she had been this way, five babies born to her in the late winter or early spring when Edgar was away and she was alone in the little cabin they had built on the *concession*. She was afraid now, afraid to lose this baby too.

It was a small house with two rooms and a low ceiling, built along the road over which trucks going to Val D'Or sped as if to evade the cold. There was cold everywhere.

Edgar had said, this time, she must leave to get help. And

she had decided to leave. She took her canning jars to a neighbor's and locked the house. This baby would be born in Montréal, in a hospital. First she would stay with Anaïs and work at the job Anaïs had gotten her in Westmount, for an English lady. She would cook until June. Then Edgar would come for her and the baby when he was through lumbering for the winter. They would take the train, the three of them and return home in the summer. This time it would be different.

*

Dandelions poked through the concrete. Slowly, the middle-aged woman boarded the train at Bonaventure Station, Edgar at her side. They were weary. They sat together, the two of them, their valises at their feet. For a long time, they did not speak, hands folded in their laps. The train left the city islands and entered farm country. The lilacs were fading; the daisies were in bloom.

"We have each other," he said, touching her hand.

She cried softly, "Why did it happen again? To us? Wouldn't we have loved that little boy?"

"Yes," he said. "We would have loved that boy."

Dinora

When he arrived in the morning, tired and full of sleep
after the night of work, she was not there. He tried to
remember: had she gone to Mass? They were farm people,
after all, who sowed prayers as they had sown corn and
potatoes in their villages in Canada.

In the city, they worked in the mills all night and slipped
into their cloth *pichous* in the morning, sipped tea, and
dreamed, as the sun rose above the tenements, of the day
dawning briskly and solemnly over the fields they had left
behind. They had left as one leaves one's youth, unknowing
that the leaving will be forever.

He sat, this tired man, not by the window but across the
window from the table. It was only across from the window
that Dinora would tolerate his rocking chair. Yes, there was a
better view by the window, but she added, wasn't she the
one, after all, whose family farm had dominated the ridge that
looked out on the Chaudière River? She knew about views as
well as anyone, better than most perhaps. But, placing the
chair by the window was out of the question. It only proved
how little he knew of arranging a kitchen!

When the boys awoke, he said, "Maman is at church". They
were young men grown strong and tall like maples, young
men who earned the money that made their lives more

comfortable. It was the boys' wages which had put an end to
the leanness that he and Dinora had known.

The winter sun arose, a solitary flower rising above the
city. It rose across the street, behind the aging tenements as
it rose at that same moment behind the farmhouse in Québec.
On other days, when he had been young, he had stood with
milk pails at the barn door watching the day's warmth climb
behind the smoke curling from the kitchen chimney.

At two, he awoke; he was hungry. He lay listening for
Dinora but could not discern her movements in the kitchen.
They were movements which a score of years had imprinted
in his memory. He remembered them as he remembered the
rising sun.

For years, he had awakened as she was leaving for work at
three. They worked these years, it seemed to him, because
they were in the habit of working.

"Dinora," he often said, "let's move to the country. Let's
buy land." They had money now like people have root cellars
filled with two years' provisions, so full that some of it will
surely go bad before it can be eaten. He was afraid
sometimes that their dollars, like onions and squashes, would
spoil.

"*Non, jamais,*" she said. "*Pas moi, jamais.*"

That afternoon, Dinora was not home. In the icebox, there
was no supper. Every night, she prepared supper for Ulysse
and the boys. It was then that he first thought that something was wrong. Perhaps he should call her sister, Florianne.
No. He could imagine Dinora, standing big, imperious, saying
he was too jumpy.

Instead he called the French hospital.

"*Non, monsieur.* They had not admitted anyone of that
description." Then he called the American hospital.

"No, sir. They had not admitted anyone of that
description."

He ate. Other days, Dinora would be leaving for work.
Today, she was a tree missing from the yard.

At three-thirty, he called the mill. "*Non,* Ulysse. She isn't in." He sat at the table, and for the first time, formed the thought, She is gone.

Where had she gone?

When would she come back?

Across the way, he could see Mme Theriault preparing supper. He had seen her preparing supper this way for more years than he had fingers. He went to the rectory. *Non*, she had not been to Mass. *Non*, he must not worry.

All night, he thought of her as he tended the looms which clanged and banged about him. Had she come back? Surely, he would find her in the kitchen in the morning. She would explain what had happened. Out of the gritty windows, he saw the lights from the city across the river. The city was asleep. His woman surely was asleep at home. In the morning, there was no sign of her. Nothing had been touched in the kitchen. The bed was made as he had left it.

He sat impatiently with his tea. Why wasn't she home? Why was she doing this?

Non, Ullysse. Dinora had not been here, said Florianne. *Non*, she was not hiding anything from him. *Oui*, of course, there had to be some explanation.

He went home again and could not sleep. He must sleep. He was a working man. He must not slack off at his job. He must continue to contribute to their savings. They were her savings too, but he felt sure she would not have touched them.

At noon, just to be sure, he went to the bank and spoke to his niece, Louis' girl who had gone through high school. "Two days ago, *ma tante* Dinora withdrew half of your account," she told him.

He walked around the city. He wept. He was exhausted. He asked himself, "Why had she done such a thing?" It was true that they did not always speak, that they often supposed things of each other. Why couldn't things have been different? Why hadn't she said something? He tried to think if she had said something.

If she came back, he would try to make things different.

They would not quarrel. He would not scoff at her; he would not say that she was satisfied with rubbing and scrubbing and spring and fall cleaning, her *grands ménages*.

If only she came back, things would be different.

She did not come back.

In the evening, the boys said, "What will we do?" They had never known a home without her. A home without Maman was as inconceivable to them as a year without a summer.

He thought, You will get your own women, and I will be alone. He was alone now. He was frightened.

For twenty years, he had not been alone. He would have to keep house, cook, and clean. He would have to learn to do woman's work. People would look strangely at him because he had no woman. They would say, "What did he do to make her leave?" Once he had promised in church that he would stay with her. Like a dumb animal, a dog, he had stayed close to her all the years that she had made him take his shoes off in the hallway.

She too promised she would stay with him. The priest said they were one. One as the night and the day, the winter and the summer. Now she was gone. He was not one anymore.

He wished now that the score between them was more even. He wished he had said more when she bought too many things, new chair covers, the latest kitchen appliance. He should have said no when she said it was her money she spent. He should have pointed out that she called the money she spent hers and the money he earned theirs. Why had he been so quiet?

The week passed. Dinora did not write; she did not call. There was no word from her. She had been a wild animal, a penned-in doe. In the night, she had broken loose and fled. She had not remembered the twenty years they had spent together, the twenty years which had not domesticated her.

He did not understand how she had left her dishes, her rugs, her new bedroom set. He did not understand how she had left her afghans, her dresses, her soaps and powders.

He would not take her back. She was a weed that bore him

no fruit. But, she did not come back.

In the night, he thought of lying with her. He thought of passing his hands over her body, of being with her. The last time they had been this way was when his niece, Louis' girl, had married. They had drunk a lot and he had felt young again. He had forgotten for a night all the nights they had gone to sleep without speaking or touching. That night, she became once again the woman he had pursued when his hair was full and black. He thought, Tonight, I love not in a dream but with my own Dinora. In the morning, they had awakened as usual. He had gone to the eight-o'clock Mass while she prepared dinner. While she was at the 10:30 High Mass, he had watched over the dinner.

Now it was he who prepared dinners. At first, like a faithful dog continuing his absent master's rounds, he prepared meals Dinora had prepared. Then he began going to cookbooks and collecting recipes. His friends teased him. They said he was like a woman inside. He thought, Yes, I am like a woman inside. What Dinora was outside, I am inside now. His friends did not understand. They still had their women. One day, he moved the kitchen table and placed the rocking chair by the window. He took the filmy curtain down and sat where he could see out. The air, the sun, the infrequent greenness were there for him at last. He sat happily for a long time.

The snow was melting. The maple sap was flowing. He knew the time had come to leave the city, to leave the world that Dinora had bound him to. Soon he would break free.

II

When he stepped out of the farmhouse, onto the granite steps, full of plans for the day, he stopped to look at the snow drops pushing through the gray matted ground in the corner of the kitchen ell. As he did so, he felt strength shoot through him, strength that rose like the maple sap. Because of these five years on the farm, there was again more than he needed of strength.

In the deep of the land which received the frost sliding
from the orchards and corn fields, there was a pond with
trout. It was a large, blue pond, below the house, so that
skating you could see only smoke curling from the solid
kitchen chimney and you could not see the house itself. The
pond was reached by a farm road. Next to the pond, Ulysses
and the boys had built an icehouse. The ice they stored there
was sold in the city all year long. In the summer, they sold
vegetables from the tailgate of their truck and at corner
stores.

He stood on the kitchen steps. It was a beautiful farm.
Wasn't this farm, this land, his woman now?

He knew where Dinora was, but he had not told the boys. A
friend who was a buyer for one of the mills had seen her. She
had aged, his friend said, but Ulysse silenced him before he
could go on. Dinora did not belong in his life now. Ulysse
said he had resown his hopes and he did not want her
memory pushing up among them like a weed. For twenty
years, she had taken hold of his life and had made it over
into hers. He never wanted that to happen to him again.

He was afraid too of having his anger come back, the
anger which would consume the energy he wanted to lavish on
his farm.

His friend thought Ulysse was as cold as the ice he and
his boys sold. He wondered what Ulysse had done to drive his
woman away.

Now when Ulysse thought of her, as he did this morning as
he looked lovingly on his fields and woods, he thought how
she would have had none of this beauty that shimmered and
vanished before you could grasp it. He had grown used to not
having a woman. He felt it no longer bothered him that one
day the boys would have women of their own and he would be
alone. The boys were looking for women. They were young
men, and he wanted them to meet French girls. Because their
town was a Yankee town, Ulysse sent the boys into the city
where the Canadians lived. On Saturdays, Alphonse and Léon
sold produce in town and at night they slept at his mother's.

In town on Saturday nights, there were dances and *soirées* filled with Canadian girls. On Sundays mornings, when he awoke, he was alone in his house. It was not possible for him to get to Mass. There was no church for him in the Yankee village. At first, he did what the *habitants* did in Canada when the snow was too deep to reach town and the cold too thick to make one's way through it: he recited the rosary in his kitchen during the hour of Mass. Later, he had taken to walking outside as he recited his beads. Now, on Sunday mornings, he put his snowshoes on and walked around his farm. Sunday was his day of leisure, and it gave him great pleasure to spend the day alone with his land. It was fertile ground into which he had sown a new life. It had become his woman. It was the only woman he had; the only woman he wanted.

That day, they worked in the sugar house as they had many days that year and the years before. The sun was warm. Each man tended to his tasks.

Across the five-acre field where he grew corn, he saw a taxi pull up around the main house. From the sugar house, they could not see where the taxi stopped.

Ulysse walked across the field; a spring breeze stroked his face gently and passed through his hair. When he reached the taxi, the driver said, "She's in there," pointing to the kitchen.

She, the *she* who had caused him the pain, whom he had not wanted to see again, ever, stood in his kitchen, her feet dripping on the linoleum.

"*Bonjour,* Ulysse," she said.

It was the same voice that had insisted shoes were to be left in the hallway, the voice that had whispered for half their savings.

"*Bonjour.*"

"Ulysse, I want to come back home," she said slowly, sounding as if she had rehearsed this line many times.

Again, she stood silent.

"It was stupid of me to go. I can't explain it, why I did it, but I want it to be over. I want to come home.

"Your home is in Lowell."

She looked up, startled. "You knew I was in Lowell?"

"*Oui.*"

Strangely, he was not angry with her. She stood in his kitchen, looking down pitifully at the pool of water that was forming at her feet. For a moment, he wished she were someone else. He knew he would have comforted anyone else who looked as she looked just then. But, because of what was between them, he did not.

He said, "We missed you very much, but that was long ago."

She leaned against one of the oak chairs she had bought 25 years before. It did not squeak under her great weight. About chairs and appliances, she knew a great deal.

They stood silent one before the other. How often in the past he had thought of this moment when he might mow her down with angry words of how she had forgotten her bonds to him and to the children that had come from them. But, he only stood silent, feeling sad that they had had the lives they had had. Unexpectedly, he felt a great loneliness for a woman. He felt a yearning to rest inside a woman he loved. Then she said, meekly, "I still have the money I took. You can have it all back. I've got more than I started with."

He stood silent. It had always been this way between them. He had always defended himself with silence.

Like the bell that had rung out to envelop her mother's funeral procession, her voice was mournful. "What will I do? What will I do?" And Ulysse remembered the choking fear he had had as the hearse crossed the cemetery gates.

She had borne his sons, and he felt vulnerable before her sorrow. How can a man forget a woman he has loved, a woman into whom he has sown life?

Then she stood straight and wiped her eyes. "Ulysse," she said, "I'm sorry for the pain I have caused you. There is no excusing what I have done. I hope someday you will forgive me. May I see the boys?"

"If you can find them. They are gone. We quarrelled. They

have left."

"You have every reason to want to hurt me," she said. "I will be at Florianne's house. You might tell them that." She walked past, turned around, and said, "I was not always a good woman for you, but I was not always a bad one either."

The door banged behind her. He stood at a window and watched the taxi roll away. He did not wave. She sat on the back seat, wiping her eyes, her head held high.

For five years, he had kept a mean image of her before him, and now like the snow on the roof that crashed to the ground, there was only the memory of a broken woman.

Slowly, he walked across the field to the sugar house where the boys were waiting for him. On Saturday morning, he would perhaps tell them about Dinora's visit. They might see her on Sunday morning if they wanted to. They were men now; he could not make decisions for them. He would just say that he did not want her or her memory around the farm.

The boys wanted to know who had come.

"A stranger," he said for now. "She was looking for someone she thought lived here."

PART II

The Life They Chose

"Some people don't remember," I could hear my mémère
saying as I stood at the edge of the road looking down the
driveway, but I could not remember what it was that people
did not remember, nor when it was she had said that about
people. But I could feel the heat of the day when we planted
the nut trees and the smell of the earth reaching up to us,
and my wanting to touch her, to have her put her arm around
me.

At the head of the driveway, beams and boards, naked in
the sun, had once been a barn and now they were heaped
high. Above, at the roof line, aluminum sheets jutted out over
the breach as if some battle had been waged at the farm. I
looked through the hole in what had been a continuous set of
buildings out to a high line of forest, capping the ridge
beyond the county road.

The wide, heavy door of the shed next to the house was
rolled back and, through the opening, beyond the forsythia, I
saw barrels and boxes and darkness. Long forsythia shoots fell
across the shed doorway and across the granite slab step.

I closed my eyes. They were gone, the people who had filled
my childhood. Mémère and Pépère were dead; my brothers and
sisters scattered, strangers to me. My parents were living in
the city. Because we could not stay, others had come to live

in our house but I saw they had not loved it as I had loved it.

I thought, I am twelve years old again, in shorts, and sneakers, and T-shirt. I tried to remember standing at the head of the driveway, What was it like to be twelve, in the year before I went to St. Joseph's? I pictured myself sitting on that granite slab that led to the shed, reading, in the shade of the blooming forsythia.

I could hear my grandmother walking down from the apartment upstairs where she lived with my grandfather. My grandfather had retired about that time, and he spent his days cutting the lawn and reading the French newspaper.

Mémère was heavy and the sound of the broad high heels of her black, laced shoes came down loudly through the wide-board floor. I knew she was coming to plant the five saplings that leaned against the house, and for a moment I thought of slipping away, but I did not.

My father had brought the saplings back with him on Saturday when he returned from the Agway. The idea was that my father would plant them for Mémère. On Sunday, she talked to my father and Pépère about planting them, but my other mémère and pépère came to visit and every one spent the afternoon on the canvas lawn chairs under the horse chestnut. And, now, the weekend was over, and my father was at work.

After breakfast, she said, "Today's the day they go in. You can wait forever for a man to do it."

My mother said, "The children will help you when you're ready."

As my grandmother descended the stairs into the shed behind me, I sat on the granite step, reading. My brow was ridged; I was biting my lower lip. In the book, I was following a boy my age, a pioneer boy. We were skating down a sinuous river to our seventeenth-century English settlement. Behind us, wolves snarled through snapping teeth as they pursued the brave boy and me across the late North American afternoon; the predators slid over the ice, and the boy and I

knew that the skates laced to our boots were our only
advantage against the wolves. We had to survive not only for
ourselves but for the people at the settlement who needed to
be warned about an attack. Could we reach the stockade of
log houses, still too far down the river, before Mémère, with
her black, broad-heeled shoes, closed in on us?

Mémère now stood heavy and intent behind me, looking at
the nut saplings. "That Eugène is too busy. And no use
waiting for Pépère," she said, moistening her lower lip with
her curled tongue. Remembering that gesture twenty-five years
later as I stood on the roadside, I was overcome with longing
for her.

"We had nut trees," she said to me in French, the only
language she knew, "when I was a girl in Canada. My father
planted them with us. I don't know what happened to them. If
we plant these, we could have nuts. In ten years. Wouldn't
you like your own nuts?"

She must have been seventy-five that year, yet she spoke
tenaciously about the future.

"Oh, I don't know," I said to her in French. My grandfather
had given her the same answer any number of times, in that
same tone. She looked at me severely, and I wished I could
take the words and the tone back.

I tried to continue reading, but behind me Mémère was
looking at the saplings, muttering. Then she asked me to help
her. I put my book down. I knew my parents would have said,
"It's the least you can do for your mémère.".

"We'll come back for the other children," she said. They
were inside playing, my sisters in their room with their dolls
and my brothers in the kitchen with a monopoly game.

From the shed, we loaded tools into a wheelbarrow, along
with the five saplings. Looking up, I saw my grandfather
watching us from one of the upstairs windows.

I put the wheelbarrow down and waved. "There's Pépère," I
said, looking at her. He seemed to step back a bit from the
window as he waved so that he appeared only half present in
the darkness.

She did not answer me and she did not wave to him. We headed out, passed the lupines which had risen, full and tall, through the lush bed of violets. The sun was very warm and Mémère said, "We'll need water, too."

I followed her as she cut across the fresh-mown lawn in front of the house. There was a ladder lying against the granite foundation of the building because, that summer, my father had undertaken to paint the windows. My grandfather was helping him sometimes, but since his retirement early in the spring, Pépère had spent a lot of time indoors by himself or out on long walks that took him away for hours. We headed for an area where we already had mature pear trees, four of them, planted by the dairyman who had lived his life on the land that had become ours as it was to become someone else's after us.

She said, "Here in a row that matches the pear trees."

I began to dig. The sod was hard and the years of grass growth had formed a thick matting. I was only twelve and not as strong as I wanted to be. As I worked, my imagination connected with the vein my novel had tapped. I pretended that we were on the edge of the wilderness. In my imagination, my grandmother's nut saplings had made the trip from France on a ship, and our settlement needed their fruit to survive.

Ahead of us, beyond the row of pear trees, beyond the blackberry patch, beyond the small field that lined the road, a truck heavy with logs passed by. I did not like the trucks going down to the lumber mill in the village. They were noisy and clumsy, and I did not like their smell.

"My father," she said, and from the tone of her voice I knew this was important to her, "gave each of us a tree. Mine was a nut tree, and I took good care of it. Your uncle Laurier loves nuts too."

"I like nuts," I said.

"My tree was like a test."

"You were how young then?"

My hair was cut in a crewcut and I could feel the sweat on

my scalp. I scratched my head and stopped digging in order to listen to her answer. "Keep digging," she said. "We'll never finish."

She wore a cotton house dress with a belt at the waist. Her hair, held in place by a net, was in the short curls my mother set for her every Saturday evening. She said, "Oh, it was sometime before we came down. I must have been a little younger than you are now. We came down before they matured."

"When did *mon oncle* Marin go back to the farm?"

"After Maman died. The following spring." And here Mémère shook her head back and forth. "Marin didn't remember anything about those trees."

Mémère was quiet, then she said, "Some people don't remember. I remember," she said. "It was hard there."

I had dug a hole. There was a little mound of earth at my feet, and I waited, knowing that I had four more holes to dig. When she saw that I was waiting for directions, she said, "The next one would go up there and the one after that there and then there and the last one a little beyond the last pear tree."

It seemed an enormous task. I had not been shown to work with my hands although my people had always worked with their hands. My family lived on a part-time farm. We had large gardens, and my parents kept thousands of chickens. But, my father did most of the work.

I wanted to run away from the farm, from digging holes. I wanted to put my skates on and race down the river. I wanted adventure. I wanted another life, but I had to stay.

When all five holes were dug, she said, "I'll get the other children. You fill the wheelbarrow with manure," and she walked toward the house. I stood alone with the empty wheelbarrow and the holes needing filling. In my child's way, it didn't seem fair to me that I had to do this work when my brothers who were near me in age did not. I knew that they would have run away as soon as they heard her heavy steps across the upstairs floor. That was the difference between us, but I did not understand that. I simply thought it wasn't fair.

From my grandmother's bedroom upstairs, I saw my grandfather looking down at me. When I looked up, he waved. I put the wheelbarrow down and waved back.

When I returned from the manure pile, my brothers and sisters were milling around next to Mémère and with their coming my mood changed. I told them to step back, to be careful not to trample on the saplings or to knock soil back into the holes. This was my project and they were late comers. I dumped two spadefuls of manure in each hole and a spadeful of earth on top of that. I had brought flies back with me, and my coming set everybody to swatting and waving them away. My grandmother undid the string on the first burlap bag. She had a pair of scissors and she tried to loosen the knot with the sharp ends. Finally, she cut the string and placed it in her dress pocket.

My youngest sister, Paulette, who had been playing mother with my other sister, picked up a tree and dropped it in the first hole. My grandmother looked at her a moment and shook her head.

"That's not the way we do it," she said. "It has to be done the right way."

Then, Mémère handed the sapling back to Paulette. Mémère said my brother who was the oldest was to go first, then myself and my younger brother and lastly my sisters who were youngest.

My older brother wanted to know if he could go ahead and get his planting over with.

"In a moment," she said. "I want you all to close your eyes."

And after we had closed our eyes, she said, "Our Lord provides us with trees and plants and beautiful, hot weather so that we can be nourished. We ask you, *mon Dieu,* to let these trees be fruitful and to give these children good lives."

We all said *ainsi soit-il.* Then she told me to lead the

Hail Mary. I was a little embarrassed because I knew what
Mémère wanted from me and already my brothers were
dismissing me because of it. But, I had also begun thinking
that I wanted to have a fine education and that I did not
want to spend my days in a mill as Pépère had nor in a
garage as my father had after him.

My child's high voice recited the first part of the Hail
Mary and my brothers and sisters picked up with the words
"Sainte Marie, mère de Dieu...". Mémère's words trailed ours
and slowed us down so that we all finished together.

Then while she held our saplings erect, each one of us
shovelled earth back into the hole, and she signalled for us
to tamp the earth around the trunk of our trees.

She said, "Think of me when you are old and you eat nuts
from these trees."

Standing at the roadway, as I did now, looking through
the breach to the ridge several miles beyond, to the ridge
that was more forested now than when I was young, I wondered
if the new people, I had heard they only rented, ate the
nuts that we had planted with Mémère that day when it was so
hot and my brothers and sisters had been strangers to me
then just as they were strangers to me now.

"Can we go now?" my brother asked.

Mémère looked at him. "What do you have to do that is so
important?"

"Play with Dicky."

Dicky lived next door and he and my two brothers often
played together.

"Your grandfather was working in the mill at your age."

My brother did not say anything. We all knew that my
grandfather had lost sight in one eye in the mill when he
was young and he had had to compensate all his life.

"Allez-vous en," she said, waving her hand away.

"Me, too," said my younger brother.

"Oui, oui, allez-vous en," she said.

Looking up, I saw my grandfather watching us from my
grandmother's bedroom window.

My brothers ran away, the soles of their feet almost
hitting against their bottoms. I saw them going towards the
road, towards Dicky's house. My brothers always played
together although they were four years apart and I was in
between them in age.

My sisters left too, and I stood alone with Mémère. When
the others were gone, in my child's way, I wanted her to
hold me, to give me a hug, but she didn't. And I didn't hold
or hug her either.

"Laurier loves nuts," she said then. Laurier was my uncle
who was a priest. He was a measure against whom she
evaluated the rest of us. "He was your age," she said, "when
he decided to go to the *collège.*" I looked at the saplings,
standing straight in the tamped earth. I did not say
anything. I was afraid to speak. My feelings about what my
grandmother wanted from me were complicated and I had
neither the words nor the habit to talk about them.

She said, "I am the only one among my brothers and sisters
with a priest for a son. Nothing makes a mother happier,
nothing, than to have a priest in her family."

I could feel the scratches on my bare legs tingling from
the perspiration that had trickled over them.

"I'm sure your mother feels the same way."

Again I did not say anything, and she told me I could go.
All my life, I had heard how wonderful it was to have a
priest in the family. And I knew now, as I walked to the
hedgerow that lined our property and then sat on the stone
wall, that I could do what my mother and my grandmother
believed would make them happy.

The hedgerow was overgrown with trees and bushes and
ferns, and I climbed a maple tree. It was tall and there
were many close branches to make climbing easy. I stood on
the crook of a branch. From up there, I could see Mémère
standing next to the nut saplings and, beyond, the big
square house. From the road came the rumbling and then the
roar of a lumber truck making its way to the paper mill.

I blocked the truck out of my mind and thought, I'm the

lookout watching for marauding Indians, or perhaps the English, and I'm here to protect the French settlement that's like a speck at the edge of the North American forest. To the east, where the land sloped beneath the old Ben Davis apple orchard, beyond the garden, I thought I saw something, a shape, slinking toward Mémère, but it turned out to be a breeze, making its way over the land.

When I looked again toward Mémère, she was gone. I hoped she had not been carried away.

I sat in the crook of a branch and felt a great loneliness come down on me. I wanted to stop being a child, but I didn't know how. I sat a long time trying to play pioneer, but I was tired of playing alone, tired of playing something that had to be created all over again every time. I wanted to start living the life that would be mine all my life. I came down the tree and walked to the house. Behind me were pear trees in a row next to the saplings. Inside the house, my sisters were playing dolls and my mother was taking a nap. She lay on her side with her hands cupped beneath her head.

I went to the shed and pulled out bicycle from where it was resting on a pile of full grain bags the men from the Agway had delivered on Friday. There was another stack of empty burlap bags that had accumulated since then. It was hot and the chickens in the two barns smelled and there were flies.

The shed became a stable and I pulled my bicycle from the clutter and was ready to gallop across the wilderness to my friend Guy's house. Once outside, I mounted and, patting the sides of the bicycle, I said, "Ready, boy?" Then we raced down the driveway to the main road, but I came to a stop because a logging truck was barrelling down to the lumber mill.

-2-

When I arrived at Guy's, Father Michaud's green Chevrolet

was parked under the shade of the maples that lined the
driveway. Monsieur Michaud, Father's brother who drove
Father around, read tabloids from Montréal while he waited
in the car.

For a moment, I thought of going back home. I did not
want to talk to Father Michaud, but I was hot and needed a
drink and rest and so I rode into the driveway.

Father Michaud's brother looked up.

"*Bonjour,*" he said.

I answered,"*Bonjour.*"

Inside the house, Father sat at the formica-top kitchen
table, facing Madame Papineau who was pouring herself a
glass of iced coffee. She poured in quick jerking motions.
My mother said Madame Papineau was a nervous wreck, and,
when I asked my mother why, she said that some things
weren't meant to be understood by twelve year old boys.

Father Michaud was tall and thin, and his hair had a bald
spot. In the summer when he came for parish visits and we
children were at home, we slipped away, through the back
door, or up the stairs. People were uncomfortable with him
and I was not old enough then to distinguish whether it was
because he was priest or because he was himself. My father
said Father Michaud needed a good dose of a man's life and I
wondered if he meant that Father Michaud should work with
his hands like other men.

He was different, too, in another way that interested me.
He rolled his *r*'s as he spoke French. Mémère said Father
Michaud's people were Acadian, and that some very difficult
things had happened to Acadians. She said he had always
spoken like that but it was not "good French". Now I know
that we French in North America have always been obsessed
with "good" and "bad" French but then I could not imagine
that Father Michaud, who had been to school a long time,
could not speak "good French".

"But why does he speak that way?" I repeated to Mémère.

"*Les maudits anglais,*" she said.

"The damn English?"

"Yes," she said, "*les maudits anglais* scattered the
Acadians all over North America so that mothers went one
way, fathers another, leaving little Acadian children to grow
up with strangers."

I said, "Did they come from another part of France?"

"I don't know," she said.

From the kitchen doorway, I could see Father Michaud's
bald spot, like a tonsure, and then he turned around and
smiled at me.

"*Eh bien, c'est David.*" he said without rolling any *r*'s.
The shades were drawn and it felt much cooler inside.

"*Bonjour,* David," Madame Papineau said to me in a quick,
clipped voice as I stood inside the screen door, passing my
tongue over my lower lip. "Come in."

Guy was there, standing on one leg as he leaned against
the kitchen counter, and I walked up to him. Neither of us
said anything. *M. le curé* and Madame Papineau talked
politely.

On these days, it seemed to me, when the priest came,
women kept the house clean and did the dishes right after
the meals. The men were always at work. Sometimes the women
baked, but it was not necessary because Father Michaud did
not want to gain weight and would not eat.

Madame Papineau picked some playing cards from the table
and said to Guy, "Put these away." Guy took the cards and
she said, blinking her eyes, "You boys go out to play."

But, instead of going out, Guy lead me upstairs. The steps
creaked under our feet and the railing wobbled under our
hands. Upstairs, Guy had a room to himself, a room cut out
of the hallway. From the ceiling, Guy had suspended model
airplane fighters and these he commanded from the oval
braided rug. It was his headquarters, and he sat down and
began to send out orders to his air squadron. They were to
do daring night missions over Germany. His pilots, he told
me, were very brave.

I felt very lonely, sitting on the rug next to him, hearing the voices of the adults downstairs.

"You boys go out. It's too nice a day to stay in," shouted Madame Papineau in her high, straining voice.

We stood up. Guy said, "Let's go to the tree house by the river." Downstairs, I heard Madame Papineau speaking again. She was using her polite voice, the voice adults around me used when speaking to someone who had been to school a long time.

Outside, the day seemed less warm than it had been. There were clouds blocking the sun. We stood outside the front door, which faced the side yard, looking at Monsieur Michaud. He sat with a tabloid from Montréal spread across the steering wheel.

"He gives me the creeps," whispered Guy.

"Monsieur Michaud?

"No, Father Michaud."

"Why?"

"I don't know."

You had to be on your best when talking to a priest. He had been to the *collège* and then to the major seminary and knew all about psychology and grammar and things like that. And you were always afraid he'd remember your confessions. Would he, as you stood, let's say in Madame Papineau's kitchen, talking to him about school, remember how you had seen the answer on Lisette Fournier's paper but the answer was wrong and all of a sudden it made you think of the right answer? As you stood there first on one foot then on another, would he remember the confession and think, Oh, this is the boy whose eyes wander?

So we avoided him without thinking too much about it. We walked across the lawn, in front of the kitchen ell, and into the carriage house where Guy's father had assembled a work space. Guy said, "We need a hammer and a saw and nails."

We looked around for a while, but we couldn't find the hammer. "I was using it just yesterday. My father will kill me," Guy said. His father exploded into fits of anger that ended in tears and broken things.

"You go back to get water while I keep looking here," Guy

said. "We'll be thirsty."

"No. You go."

"Don't be silly. You won't know where to look."

Reluctantly, I walked out of the barn and into a shed full
of discarded household objects, an old electric stove,
cardboard boxes, trash barrels. From the steps leading into
the kitchen, I could hear Madame Papineau speaking in a loud
whisper, her voice pushed by an anger she could barely
conceal.

"*Mon père*, I'm at the end of what I can take. When we were
poor, I could deal with that. But the drinking and now, and
now..." but she did not finish what she was saying. Instead
she cried and blew her nose.

"How could this other woman be so..." and she broke down
crying again.

"When we had nothing, it was hard but we used to find ways
of making ends meet. But now this, this is too much."

I dared not move. I was ashamed to be hearing her words
and yet I was twelve and beginning to have an interest in
the things between men and women.

"And if the boys find out. What kind of an example is it
for them?"

"Things happen to us. We pull through. God does not forget
us," said Father Michaud.

"I can't be poor again," she said. "I won't be poor!"

There was a pause. I heard Madame Papineau blow her nose
again and then a chair scraped against the floor and I heard
the rattle of dishes against each other and the sound of
plates being placed in the sink. "I must see both of you at
the rectory office. Monsieur Papineau must come too."

"He will not come. He gives me money for the house and
the boys but he'll have nothing to do with me."

By then I had grown quite ashamed that I had stayed so
long listening. A black tomcat came into the shed and rubbed
against my bare legs. I dared not shove him away. I stood in
the shed immobilized by what I had heard, afraid that if I
moved I would knock into something. Then Father Michaud

would know me not only for my wandering eyes, but also for my ears that stayed to hear what was not meant for them. I could feel my face warm and full, almost bursting, and I turned around and walked out of the shed.

I waited a while and then, whistling, and walking loudly, I retraced my steps and knocked on the door.

Monsieur le curé was getting up to go. He turned to me and said, "Tell your mother I'll be up her way next Monday rather than this Friday. I'll give my blessing now."

We knelt.

And with that he left. I asked Madame Papineau for a bottle in which to carry water. Her eyes were red, and she seemed very nervous. I was embarrassed to be there.

We played all afternoon, Guy and I, in the tree house that was suspended over the river. We were playing bomber raids. I wanted to play pioneer, but Guy didn't. All afternoon, I thought about what I had heard, about how unhappy Madame Papineau was. Finally, the sun began to lose some of its intensity, and I looked up to see Madame Papineau approaching. She was standing at the crest of the rise where it levels off after its climb from the river. Beyond, so that we could not see it, was the house.

"Time for supper," she shouted.

Guy and I walked back slowly. He was full of talk that suddenly seemed childish as I thought about his mother and father, about my own mother and father and my mémère and pépère. When we reached the crest, I saw Monsieur Papineau step out of his car. He was not a tall man, not particularly handsome. I had seen tall, handsome men and I knew Monsieur Papineau was not one of these.

He worked as a bread delivery man and he stood in the yard wearing a brown outfit the company required him to wear. He waited for us and when we got there he asked Guy how he was and then me. I felt very daring to be talking to a man who had another woman. I had never known a man who had had another woman.

-3-

Those summer afternoons, when I was a child, my grandparents sat under the horse chestnut tree, on canvas lawn chairs, waiting for my father. They sat side by side, not talking, and I would think, When people have been together a long time they have said all there is to say to one other.

My grandfather made drinks, with whiskey, that he kept in an ice chest in the double shade of the horse chestnut and the picnic table. When my father came home in the summer, always after six, they sat under the horse chestnut tree on the canvas chairs and drank a glass together. Mémère said Pépère drank his income away, and it did seem he drank a lot but we always knew what to give him for Christmas and his birthday and he was never drunk. My father and his father would sit together in the shade of the tree and drink. For long periods, they would not speak and neither felt uncomfortable.

I would sit with them and I would not speak. My brothers would be playing pass on the lawn in front of us, and my sisters too would be outside doing something, with dollies. They were always playing with dollies.

My father might say, "It was hot as hell in town today."

"Staying home's not that great," my grandfather would answer.

If my grandmother were out with us by the picnic table, she might say, "You children all had a chance. Laurier didn't let things slip by."

"Laurier. Laurier," my father would say. "Laurier has no idea what life's all about."

My grandmother would turn icy but she would say nothing more.

When I got home that night, though, my grandparents were not outside and my father had not arrived from the city where his garage was in the tenement district. He often said there was no breeze where he was, not like in the village near where we lived. And it would anger him when my mother said simply, "That's where your customers are."

My mother was carrying a tray of plastic dishes and glasses out to the picnic table. The table was beneath the horse chestnut not far from where my grandmother and I had planted the nut saplings, and the canvas chairs were in a half circle to one side of the table. My sisters were sitting on the chairs, and I could tell they had just brought trays of dishes and food out to the table and I knew they were hoping my mother would not ask them again to help.

My mother looked up at me and said, "You come here, you."

I took my bicycle into the shed and put it against a feed bag. Then, I walked over to the chestnut tree. My mother was bending over the picnic table to straighten the cloth. I stopped a few feet away from her and waited for her to finish.

"If you were next to the kitchen, why didn't you bring something?" she said.

"I forgot," I said.

"Not the only thing you forgot today," she said.

"What do you mean?"

"I mean I have to know where you are," she said, without stopping her work. "You have to ask every time. Do you think I went out without asking permission from my mother or my father?"

"I tried to, but you were napping."

"You think about what you're going to do early enough to ask permission. There'll be a punishment next time."

I said I was sorry that I had forgotten to ask. She said being sorry was not enough.

My younger sister said, "I bet he didn't forget. He just thinks he's too big."

My mother said, "Mind your own business, you." And then she said to me, "It was too far to go on a hot day."

"We played by the river where it was cool."

She had her back to me now and I could see the nape of her neck where the hair was a stubble. Above that, her hair was still awry from having been lain on.

I said, "Father Michaud was there. He'll be here on Monday, he says."

"My cleaning's always done good on Saturday. Now help me with this picnic stuff."

So I helped her bring things out. I figured that it would appease her, and it did and she did not mention again my being gone without permission. She went inside to cook and she said that I could do whatever I wanted for a while. I sat down with my book about the boy who was being chased by wolves, racing down to the settlement at the edge of the river. I sat at the horse chestnut tree and read. My sisters were chattering next to me. I tried not to hear them.

My two brothers were on the front lawn playing with a bat and ball. They passed the ball back and forth, back and forth as I sat reading under the horse chestnut.

When the boy in the story arrived at the settlement, the lights of the houses scared the wolves. The pack slackened a bit. The boy screamed and doors opened as people came out with guns. They began to shoot the wolves, and the boy dashed inside with his skates still on. I figured they didn't have linoleum in those days.

I didn't get to the part where the Indians come to attack the settlement because my mother came out again with a platter of bread rolls.

"Go upstairs," she said. "Tell Mémère and Pépère that we will eat in ten minutes."

My grandparents' apartment could be approached from the front door. There were stairs there that lead to a small room off both the living room and the kitchen. Upstairs, my grandfather was sitting in the kitchen writing in an account book. He always kept records of their expenditures and, at the end of the year, he could tell almost to the penny how much they had spent on this and on that.

"*Bonjour,*" he said. "You coming to let me beat you at checkers again?"

"Time to eat in ten minutes," I said.

My grandmother was reading from her prayer book in the

living room, next to the piano where there were pictures of her children and grandchildren. Her head was surrounded by a white antimacassar. As I came in, she did not move. It was her habit to finish her prayer before speaking to anyone. I sat down where Pépère could not see me, my bare legs dangling over the horsehair couch.

Her missal was stuffed with holy pictures and obituary cards, pictures of her dead brothers and sisters and her parents. She had told me her father had died in Canada on a visit. It was a very sad thing for her to have her father buried there and her mother here. She said she and my pépère would be placed side by side. She said, "You'll be able to visit us there," but I did not want to think of that.

She looked up at last from her prayer book.

"Supper's ready in ten minutes."

She closed her eyes as if they were very tired and then she opened them up again and said, "I was talking to Father Michaud. There is some money in the parish to help boys go to the high school seminary."

"Oh," I said, my heart jumping. "They have a lot of money?"

"Some."

I sat there both knowing and not knowing what she was going to say.

"You're good at school. Sometimes, that's one way God has of telling a boy he wants him. Would you like to go to St. Joseph's like your uncle Laurier?"

I didn't know. I wasn't ready yet to say what I wanted to do.

"Laurier was real smart," she said. "They sent him to Rome to study. It must be very nice to go to Rome. The pope gave him communion once."

Pépère came in from the kitchen. "Laurier was real smart in some things, but he couldn't have made it as a businessman. Not like your father."

I looked at Pépère. He looked sure of himself as he spoke

of my father whom I hadn't thought of before as having a business.

"I can help you, too," she said, with an intensity to her voice that I had not heard before. "I have some money set aside. I will send it to the seminary every month to help pay your expenses. Would you like that?"

"I don't know what my parents would say," I answered.

"Let me ask them," she said. "They won't stand in God's way."

"Perhaps David would rather go to school around here. It would be real nice. What's wrong with the Catholic school in Lewiston?," Pépère said.

"And perhaps he wouldn't like that," Mémère answered. "Perhaps he'd like something else." There was something in her voice that I didn't understand.

"Would you like that?" Pépère asked.

"I don't know," I said. I had always thought that I would go to the seminary, le *collège*. It was where the best of the French-Canadian boys went, Mémère said.

"You have too much time on your hands," she said to him. "Why don't you garden more or paint those windows? Eugène's exhausted; he works too much. He'll never get to it."

My grandfather walked out of the room, but there was no quiet in the apartment. Then he returned and stared at her for a long time. I got up and looked at a daguerreotype of Mémère's family in Canada. It was brown and round like a chimney-hole cover. Then I heard Pépère say in a low crisp voice, "Perhaps you would like to go visit your sister in Connecticut for a while, Florianne?"

He walked back into the kitchen. They each sat silently, she in the living room with her missal bursting with holy cards in her lap, and he with the ledger sheets around him on the table.

They remained silent for a long time, and I wandered into my grandmother's bedroom and looked out to the nut trees. Someday, when I was big and grown up, the saplings would be bearing fruit, I realized, and I would remember the day they were planted. But, I did not know that I would remember so much of what else had happened. Then I came back and stood between them looking at the coleus plants that grew on a table next to me. Finally, I said, "It's time to eat," and I turned around and went downstairs.

I felt as if I were running away.

My mother was making iced tea. She looked up. "All set?" she asked.

Pépère did not join us. While we were eating, Mémère said he was having a hard time getting used to retirement. She said he wanted to eat alone, upstairs. I raised my eyes but I did not see him looking down at us from any of the windows. I thought that it would be nice to play checkers with him later.

My father did not say anything. After we had eaten, Mémère spoke to my parents about my going to St. Joseph's. My brothers were playing ball on the lawn, passing the ball back and forth, back and forth. My sisters were inside, playing with their dollies.

I sat quietly as my mother and father and mémère chose the life I should lead.

My Call to be David

St. Joseph's was like a greenhouse at noon with the full heat of the sun on it. Later it seemed there hadn't been enough water or shade there for me, but then I didn't know that, at least just yet.

The Amorists demanded a lot from us: read this handout; perform that extra experiment; translate two more pages. And I did it all. I was a materialist of the intellect.

Around me, other boys were taking St. Joseph's in stride, looking for corners to cut; but I was like the founder of the Amorists: I was a zealot. I liked the pace we maintained. Sometimes the other boys said I made things harder for them, but I did not believe in letting opportunities slip by.

My uncle Laurier had been very circumspect when we had talked about his alma mater. He had only said then that I would have a try at a fine college preparation. So I had asked, "You're glad you went?" and he had said yes but he would not say anything else about the Amorists.

The Amorist congregation (it had been founded in the last century in Québec) had sent my uncle to Rome for his scholasticate studies.

Neither my father nor my grandmother could remember what it was the Amorists had been preening Laurier for in Rome, nor why he had left the congregation to become a diocesan priest.

However, Father Sanscoeur, our principal, seemed to remember well why my uncle, who was his classmate, had left. He made allusions to men who lacked the courage to bear their crosses.

"Pride," he said, the only time I asked him what my uncle's cross might have been. I thought it odd that Sanscoeur had said that because he himself, I was sure, was a prideful man, proud of the things he had gathered around him, proud of his opinions. I did not like him; there was something implacable interposed between us, but I could not name it. I had not had enough experience of the world then to know what it was that set us one against the another, but I was soon to have more experience.

In my Fourth Form, my senior year, the faculty created an honor society. We were a very small school and a group further distinguishing some boys from the others could only serve to increase the hothouse atmosphere. In fact, the St. Joseph's Society had been much talked about for weeks.

On the evening of the initial inductions, André Cyr who was a real plodder had said, "Of course, you'll make it. Who else is going to if you don't?"

And it was true. In spite of my discomfort with Sanscoeur, of my sense of something implacable between us, I knew he would have to include me. I was the one, after all, who read the extra page, wrote the extra paragraph, learned the extra vocabulary. I was a gutsy kid in that way. I was out to make the most of my opportunities.

My uncle Laurier too had made the most of things. My grandmother was very proud of him. He was the standard against whom she measured the rest of us.

Sitting in the auditorium that evening of my final year at St. Joseph's, I was aware of my nervousness about having to get up in front of a school where the hothouse environment seemed to have favored me over others. I knew that many resented me for this.

Sanscoeur called out last names alphabetically and the boys

walked up to the stage. I'm David Soucy, and I knew just
when Sanscoeur would call me.

But, he did not call me.

Georges Tellier is who he called instead of David Soucy.
That's when everyone snickered and turned around.

Father Sanscoeur, fat and smug on the stage proscenium,
paused a moment, too long it seemed to me, and then
continued to read the names of the St. Joseph inductees. I sat
with a smile which was held in place with every ounce of
pride I had as my mind raced to find the right words for
what was happening just then.

Up on stage Father Sanscoeur finally finished and then
looked around the room. His big black cassock swayed gently
as he rocked in front of the drawn curtains.

I clutched the seminarian's cross which hung from a long
black cord set around my neck, but I was not aware of what
I was doing. I was only aware of the boys staring at me and
of the interminable pause during which Sanscoeur looked
around the room.

Then he said, "That's it. You may congratulate the nominees
by applauding."

We were just one hundred and fifty boys at the edge of
the forest. Beyond the darkened window panes, I could not see
the woods, but I was wishing I could run away and hide there,
hide and never come back to Sanscoeur and to the boys
around me who counted class averages in miserly fashion and
did not forgive you if you were ambitious for something
different for yourself, if you loved words and caressed them
and offered them for all to hear.

Then or later, I couldn't get away at all, couldn't hide
where no one would see me, where I could go for a while as
a dog goes into a barn cellar or into a forest to lick a wound
clean.

*

The next day, I sat with my classmates in the gray Fourth-
Form classroom, by a large window overlooking the religious
grotto. At that time of year, the sun shone through the

maples and played with the shadows of bare branches on the
stones of the altar and the railing.

Father Dubé spoke of the honor conferred to the few
inducted into the St. Joseph Society. I felt ashamed, deeply
ashamed, just as I had the evening before in the bare
auditorium. This time my classmates did not turn to look at
me nor did they whisper my name.

What had I done wrong, what had I not done enough of?
And even as I was thinking these thoughts, I sensed they
would not provide the right answer.

I considered leaving St. Joseph's that very day, quitting.
Getting up perhaps in the middle of Dubé's lecture on *la
preciosité* and telling them all to go to hell. My uncle Laurier
had left, but I couldn't do it just then: I had aways wanted to
be an Amorist, to be a priest, had always felt the vocation to
be an intermediary between God and Human. *How was I to
reach that goal if not through the Amorists?*

When I imagined telling my parents how I had gotten up in
the middle of class and had shouted out, I knew my father
would say I had let my chances slip by. He would remind me
that my uncle Laurier had not let go of opportunities before
he had made the most of them. My uncle had, after all, been
sent to Rome.

And besides, I thought, looking out on the sun playing
through the bare maples in the grotto, I could have done all
my screaming in the auditorium, could have done it with so
much more show in front of all the boys and all the faculty.
Dubé and my fellow Fourth Formers seemed small consolation
compared to that. So, I did not get up and shout out.

Instead I thought of my mémère, who had said working in
the mills had been like being in a coffin all those years, who
had done it so that her children and grandchildren would have
opportunities. She would say that Sanscoeur was a priest,
after all, with a fine education, an Amorist, and I, I was only
a boy, a boy who had been passed over, who had let his
chances slip by.

In the front of the classroom, Dubé was saying, "The best

writers and artists of the time, of course, rose above *la préciosité*. Molière even wrote some of his finest comedies in mockery of those who choose form over substance."

Suddenly, I knew what I would have to do. I would storm over to Father Sanscoeur's office to demand an explanation, demand to know why André Cyr and Georges Tellier had been selected while I who was like the founder had been passed over.

I would demand an apology.

-2-

I had my visit with Sanscoeur.

He sent a message that I was to come right after afternoon classes.

I stood in the dark, narrow hallway, leading to his office, clutching the seminarian's cross that rested on my shirt front. That cross which as an Amorist seminarian I had earned in my first year would be at the center of what was to happen to me that afternoon. But, I did not know that then as I waited in the dark hallway for something, waited as the Church waits for the breath of the spirit, for divine inspiration, to announce itself to me. Breathing deeply, I forced my hand to strike against the door. The *oui* that rumbled out of the superior's office triggered a response and I turned the handle. Slowly the door opened. For a moment, I was disoriented by the light. Involuntarily, I focused on the large mouth of teeth set in the corpulent cheeks. Between the teeth was a cigar.

If the highly-polished floor of the hallway could have swallowed me up just then, I would gladly have been swallowed up. I knew that, in the little room, surrounded by Sanscoeur's things, I would not shout and rage and demand an apology. Instead, I would sit in the stuffed wing-back chair listening to Sanscoeur, wishing I could produce an extravagant gesture and knowing that I would not.

These sessions always began with a smile, a polite hand

gesture toward the stuffed chair re-upholstered over the summer. We were after all civilized, cultured people, Sanscoeur seemed to imply. "And, your father is still at the same plant?"

"He runs a garage," I said.

"Oh, yes, of course," he answered. "And your mother?"

My mother, I thought, my mother wishes she had this elegant wing-back chair I'm sitting on. I did not say that of course, but I remembered the founder who was a zealot.

Instead, because I was a trusting boy then, a boy who wanted to believe in goodness, a boy ill-suited to this struggle with Sanscoeur, I would not say such a thing to this priest who had taken a vow of poverty, who had forgotten that he had come from the same world as I.

Sitting in a room full of books, a room such as there were none in my parents' home, I would forget that between Sanscoeur and me there was an implacable thing I could not name, a thing that was very unlike me, unlike the me that I would struggle to become all my life. I would forget just then that I knew about the implacable thing between us, forget because I wanted to forget, needed to forget. And so I would think that, this time, Sanscoeur and I would talk, I sitting here and he sitting there, son and father, and Sanscoeur would touch something in me and I would open up, blossom like a crocus out of the cold earth once it is touched by the sun.

But, soon, instinctively, I looked out the closed window, through the draw drapes, toward the Protestant cemetery. The last of the leaves danced in the breeze that would soon pull them loose from their branches. I tried to focus on something outside of Sanscoeur's office, something else, something bigger than leaves, something true and beautiful. I focused on a maple; the maple was big and bare. It stood there stark and empty.

The superior's voice droned on. He was not speaking to me, I thought, but to some other boy in the luxurious stuffed chair, a stupid, vulgar boy. Surely, Sanscoeur was not now

calling me by name, was not now implying that I, David
Soucy, who more than anything wanted to be fine but did
not know how, was that boy.

"David! Are you listening to me?" he asked, his voice
rumbling through the layers of flesh.

"*Oui, mon père,*" I said, as my left hand clutched my
seminarian's cross. I gathered my energy and focused on
Sanscoeur.

Behind and to the side of him, the walls were lined with
books. I thought, Someday I will read books until there are
no more words left to read. I believed then in the power of
words, I who came from a family that did not believe in the
power of words.

Meanwhile I heard crazy words that only confused me.

"So you want to be an *artiste!*" he said, and unbelievably I
felt myself relax. I knew that Sanscoeur too had come from a
family that did not believe in words, that still worked in the
mills. I thought, He understands. He will be my father and
guide.

And then the sound of his voice which had been ringing in
my ears became clear and I realized he had flung, cast out,
the word *artiste*, so that *artiste,* that fine role I was striving
to fulfill, had always dreamed of becoming, just as I had
always dreamed of being a priest as my uncle Laurier was,
this word *artiste* might as well have been *atheist.*

I felt the words, "Go to hell!" whelm up in me. I was only a
minor seminarian though and he, he was a priest, a man with
a fine education, an Amorist such as my mémère and my
father and my mother held in example before me. So, I did
not say anything.

"The congregation has no need for part-time priests, for
littérateurs," he said. He pronounced the word *littérateurs*
as if he had compressed it into four letters, uttered it in the
accented way the French from France might have uttered it,
the French from France that we French of North America
have always loved and hated. I knew then what he was telling
me, that I took myself to be something of a French from

France, that I took myself to be better than those around
me. It was obvious then that he was about to state something
to me that I would not like and that he had not called me in
to apologize for his stupidity of the previous evening.

"I don't feel you are worthy to wear your seminarian's
cross" was what he said.

His fat, indulgent hand reached out over the oak desk. His
palm opened upward for me to place my cross in it. I thought,
This man is crazy. There I was, the student who asked his
teachers for extra work and he was saying I wasn't enough
somehow, not measuring up. If not me, who else could he
possibly be looking for to preen and to nurture and to water
in the noonday sun?

"Please take off your cross and give it to me. I will keep
it," he said, "until you change your ways."

He continued to hold his hand out for me to place the cross
there in his open palm, but I did not move. I was like one of
those startled deer immobilized in the beam of a head light. I
examined my shoes and the pattern on the rug. I still
remember the pattern: it was a thick green rug with a border
of arabesque designs. Beneath the rug was a highly-polished
wide-board oak floor. Across from me was a lovely, hardwood cabinet. It held two shelves of records and above this
large collection was a hi-fi. There was a record resting on the
turntable. I thought, Who is this man to judge me?

In my mind was the example of the founder of the
Amorists, the first of all the Amorists, a man not unlike the
boy I was. He had been a true Amorist, as I could be a true
Amorist: I was not one who would not take his vows in
stride.

"Well!" he said, gesturing towards himself with his fingers.
He was impatient, and he might as well have said, "You
stupid boy!"

"I've done my best," I said, startled by the brusqueness of
his voice. I knew I had not done wrong, at least not in the
way one sets out willfully to do wrong.

"I'm not doubting that you've done your best," said

Sanscoeur, "but we need to help you to change your ways, don't we?"

I looked up and stared across the desk and saw dozens and dozens of books. I was confused. There were books everywhere.

I looked from the superior, to the cigar stub smoldering in an ashtray between us, to the maples, bare and stark, among the graves, and beyond to the forest. Then, slowly, my eyes focused on Father Sanscoeur's demanding outstretched hand.

Slowly, mechanically, so that later I hardly remembered doing it, I slipped the long black cord and the brass cross from around my neck. I was overcome with shame. I had worn the cross for three years and I felt as if I were undressing, there in front of the superior. I placed the cross in Sanscoeur's hand, and he placed it on his desk, out in the open, for all to see, to gasp at the horror of it, as one might gasp at the head of John the Baptist, served on a tray, right there on the superior's cluttered desk. My head, the head of a person who wasn't good enough to be an Amorist.

I looked down at the floor. I wanted to scream, to cry, to spit in Sanscoeur's face. How could my parents, how could my mémère, understand that Sanscoeur, and not I, was the person who was lacking, who did not have enough of whatever had to be enough? And regardless of what I could say, how could I be a fine man like my uncle Laurier if I did not have my cross?

-3-

That night, I awoke in a sweat, my pajamas drenched. I had dreamt I was hurrying down the long driveway from the Fathers' big, brick house to High Street when a large, expensive car bore down on me. I saw it coming, wide, heavy, but I was not able to outdistance it. I tried to run faster; the large car went faster too. I panted hard; the car narrowed the gap between us. I couldn't get away. There was a terrible smell of smoke. I tripped and, turning my eyes towards the car, I saw a wheel about to roll over my head. It was then that I awoke with a gasp: my heart beat rapidly. For a moment I lay afraid in the sweaty sheets, not knowing what was dream, what was real. It was not the first time I had had this dream, but it had never been so intense. I might have relaxed knowing that I was surrounded by my sleeping classmates, but I did not feel safe: these were the boys who would soon jeer at me for having lost my seminarian's cross.

I threw the blankets over the foot of the bed. Groping in the dark, I changed my pajamas. I placed a bath towel on the damp sheet and crawled in under the blankets to get warm. Snatches of the dream returned, first as feelings and then as images. I was still afraid; I hid in my blankets. Around me, my classmates slept quietly.

From the town docks, lights reached up into the cavernous room, casting slivers of light around the bare, dark shades. I lay like a corpse. Once again, I saw the fat, indulgent hand outstretched, palm upward.

How would I dare now to write in the dormitory at night as I lay on the bed waiting for lights-out or during the day when I went to the Fourth-Form classroom by myself? How would I dare when all around me boys would be repeating mockingly, "He thinks he's an *artiste,* a *littérateur,* but he does not have his cross. He has been passed over"?

Then, breathing a deep breath, I arose and a shiver worked its way up and down my spine. I thought happily, I haven't been run over; I am a living person.

I walked slowly between beds, knocking lightly into slippers. Someone mumbled in his sleep. Quietly, I made my way through the dark dormitory. Down I went, down the stairs, the treads solid and not creaking, not giving me away to Dubé nor to Sanscoeur. I made no noise, not in the hallway downstairs, next to the refectory, not even as I turned into the vestibule by the chapel. The chapel was full of the strong smell of wax. Up to then, I had been in small narrow passages and now I was in a large, open space. I breathed a deep breath and walked toward the sanctuary. Its lamp cast a flickering light across the front of the room.

Kneeling in front of the statue of Mary, I began to recite the Hail Mary. The words slipped out on their own, like so many words I had spoken already in my life, words of every kind that were someone else's words. I had been told that Mary would always be there for me, but like so many other things I had been told it was not true just then.

I stopped praying. The chapel was very quiet. Whenever I stopped using other people's words, there was always stillness, a withered silence. I felt so inadequate. How was I to be a priest, an intermediary between God and Human, if I could not even pray? How could there be any other way?

Where were they, the people like me, the *artistes*, the *littérateurs*, who were zealots as the founder had been, who would show me how to live my life as Sanscoeur could not? The people who would not leave me silent at the foot of the wooden statue, who would teach me to make words that only I could make?

I was young, but I felt old, wilted, parched. Like a plant smothered by weeds, I felt crowded out by people like Sanscoeur and André Cyr. How could I who had not yet borne fruit feel as if I were going to seed?

The room was cold and empty. I felt like one of the diminutive nuns who worked in our kitchen. They whispered to each other and did not look at us, turning away to hide. They had sacrificed their lives.

I felt exhausted, but I did not want to give my life away. I was young and I had not yet lived. Praying to the statue was like talking to Sanscoeur. I needed something else in my life. Abruptly I stood up and crossed the sanctuary, pulled by a longing that I could not explain to myself. I went through the sacristy and entered the library from the back. At that end of the room, the librarian had a collection of plants and these were kept under a grow-light which cast shadows over the brick walls and the wooden shelving. I had always been happy in this room. There was a hush here, a feeling of quiet and peace.

"Oh, the books!" my mémère had said when I first walked
through the library with my family. "Isn't this just what you
want! You and Laurier, you're so alike, you!"

It had been, yes, what I had wanted, this room where,
unknown to me, in some way, I had been creating what there
was of myself. Standing there, in the back of the library, I
could feel my shoulders drop.

Slowly, I found myself walking down the wall of books to
my right, passing my index finger along the spines until I
reached the French novels section. There on a shelf near the
top was a book that I pulled out. On the inside front cover
was a book plate written in French: "French prize. Awarded
to David Soucy. June 1963."

The plate was one of many commendations that I had
received in my three years at St Joseph's. Someday boys who
had never met me would read those book plates, and they
would see that I had been a special boy. They would not know
that I had been passed over by Sanscoeur and that I had had
to give him my cross so that it lay in his hand like the head
of John the Baptist, there out in the open for all to see, the
head of an unworthy boy.

And there had been other prizes -- in English, in history,
in Latin -- but now the fantasy of boys someday reading the
book plates bearing my name was suddenly not enough, not
enough for the *artiste,* the *littérateur,* that I was. I needed
more. I needed, I knew now, to create my own words, words
that would come from me as water from the earth, as a plant
from the seed. It was my own words that I needed, but
needed not on these shelves for some future boys. The words
I needed were words for myself.

And I needed to live a life that made loving words possible.

In a moment, I understood why I had come to St. Joseph,
understood why I was going to leave.

I began to laugh. I laughed in idiotic spasms and tears
began to form in the corners of my eyes.

"The artist is a priest," I said incredulously. This thought
was like a rain falling on a dry land, or a cloud covering a

noonday sun.

I felt my chest opening. It was as if some constricting cord that had tied me to something had suddenly been slipped off and now I could breathe more easily.

It seemed so simple: needing words of my own and knowing that an *artiste,* wasn't he someone who wasn't himself sometimes, the self who was fat or thin, young or old, male or female but was someone who stood timeless? The artist was a priest, a person who stood in a special way between God -- as I called it then -- on the one hand and his own temporal self and the world on the other?

I paced the length of the room. "The artist is a priest," I said over and over again, knowing for the first time that I did not have to become an Amorist to become the priest I was striving to become.

As I articulated the decision that had already taken shape within me, I paced up and down and felt myself relax. I felt incredibly awake, alive as my fantasy created spaces in which I could form a future. I ceased to be obsessed with Sanscoeur and began to grope for the words of the young man I was, dreaming dreams I had not dared to dream before.

PART III

Need not Apply

Everything at our place seemed too green, too lush. The
forest was creeping in from the edges of the fields where it
had once been contained by stone walls. Even the foundation
hole to the old cattle barn had little trees growing in it.

The barn had collapsed before we bought the farm. The first
summer, we cleared the foundation hole with a bonfire. I'd
like to say we invited all our friends and had a good time,
but the truth of it was that we didn't know many people
around here and, much of that year, we were very isolated.
So, when we put a match to the barn ruins, it was to the
volunteer fire fighters that we served lemonade.

That year was a hard year. Right after we had committed
ourselves to a mortgage, the government funds for Richard's
city job were cut. So he stayed home with the kids while I
took on some waitressing. I worked in a restaurant in the
village. We served breakfast and workingmen's lunches. The
men left small tips: they didn't have any more money than we
had. Richard and I didn't get ahead that winter.

That cold, interminable winter melted into spring and then,
although it was summer, things, the things that would have
made a difference to our lives, did not materialize for us as
we had hoped they would when winter had at last given way
to the warmer days of spring. We planted a large garden, and

Richard was really good at tending it. He sold seedlings and produce. The florists bought some of our flowers. It was promising, but we needed more than promise.

And now it was October again and when I looked out -- I was still in my bathrobe and slippers -- I saw a flock of grosbeaks. There were quite a number of them in the half-bare trees, their forms clearly delineated. I walked up to the window above the sink. I would have said that I was really quite noiseless about it, but the flock took flight as if I had shoo-ed them away.

Grosbeaks, I thought. For heaven's sake, everybody knows you don't get winter birds in your cherry trees until it's winter, and we were just barely out of summer! It seemed like a symbol, more cold coming into my life!

I said, "Paulette, cool it. Don't get so goddamn symbolic. They're only winter birds taking flight." But, I had been nurturing a hope all morning and then, when I saw the grosbeaks take flight, it was as if the anxiety I had been keeping under control morning began flapping inside of me.

"You're going to look good," I said. "That's one thing that's for sure."

I had already decided on my outfit. I was glad, too, because I was getting so nervous I don't think I could have dressed myself decently that morning. Actually I couldn't have gone wrong by much because I really had only two outfits-- one summer and one winter one. The rest was just odd stuff that I could sometimes match. Anyway, for mid-day in mid-October, I had done what I thought was a clever combination of summer and winter clothing by putting the skirt of one with the blouse of the other.

When I stepped out of the house later, like Cinderella in the open-toed shoes my narrow-footed sister-in-law had given me, the grosbeaks, those birds of cold and ice had returned to the cherry trees. I tried to shoo them away; I tried to wave my arms to scare them off, but they stayed right there on those branches.

Richard and the children had walked out with me, and

Richard gave me a good hug and he said, "You look terrific."

Well, it was going to take more than looks, I said, but I appreciated his giving me an ego boost. We both had a lot to win from this. So I started the car. The engine turned over once and another time and, when it sparked alive, I was one hell of a relieved woman. Sometimes, the only thing that got the car going was a jumpstart with cables. When we had grown up here, not in the village where we live now but in places like it, we hadn't realized we were poor. We had worked hard to get educations that were now useless to us in some fundamental way.

"You'll do great," said Richard.

"If I can get there," I answered. Struggling with the car day after day was starting to get to me. I never knew when I'd get stranded at a stop sign.

So the kids waved and Richard waved and I waved and then I was backing out of the driveway and the dog was barking. I thought, I'll either drive out every day like this or this is the one and only time, a perfect waste of my morning.

The sun was warm, and I was still fresh from my bath. As I sang notes from a Copland composition playing on the radio, I could feel myself grow calmer. For a while, I felt like a normal person and not like a woman who was caught in something that felt like a melodrama. It did seem a lot like the soap operas that I didn't watch on TV -- except that I wasn't at all sure that my own story would come out ok. We were, after all, in the throes of a recession.

All along the way, I went ooh and aah at what was left of the maples -- some of them still deeply red and yellow and full. The oaks were just beginning to turn russet, a color which never elicits quite the same ooh and aah, but they were still full of leaves. The sun shone through the foliage making it bright, and I thought that my Maine was very beautiful. I had been born here and I had been away and something had drawn me back. But it was only October and I was trying very hard not to think of another winter with the drafts blowing around our feet, a winter with our wearing

last year's boots, a winter filled with dread that the car
would not start and the pipes would freeze.

I was placing many hopes on this job interview, but I was
also afraid of being disappointed one more time. The
competition for jobs had grown fierce. There was always
someone from out-of-state who had done the very thing for
umpteen years in Massachusetts or Connecticut and was sure,
according to the newspaper profile that followed his or her
employment, that Maine's quality of life compensated for the
low salary. And I thought, Low salary, give me a break! At
one point, I caught myself thinking of how I would spend it
all: a newer car that didn't always break down, all kinds of
new wool for sweaters, scarves, and mittens, and new pants
for both Richard and myself -- we were still wearing
bellbottoms that had gone out of style several years before.
You know, bellbottoms that had the bottoms sewed in to look
like straight pants. But the look was a little on the made-over
side. Oh! but I was tired of the made-over side of my life.

When at last I got into the city, I felt like a stranger to
myself, a professional stranger in heels driving to an
appointment through busy, downtown streets. The arts-council
building was not difficult to find, and I fell in love with it
immediately. It was a Victorian structure that stood beneath
tall elms, and its foundation was behind a wide bed of pansy,
petunia, and African marigold. Everything was clean and
spacious. To the left of the building, there was a parking lot
discretely hidden behind a thicket of rose bushes.

I should have parked down the street -- or even around the
corner -- so that, if I had any trouble with the car, I could
jump start it without letting everyone in the arts council
know about it. But, I just didn't think of that. Before I knew
it, I was parked in the lot, feeling very much at home,
wanting it to be taken for granted that I belonged in a place
just like this.

And the office, it took my breath away! Natural-finish
wainscoating and plants and hardwood floors. And everything
plumb and square. I want it, I thought. I want all of it!

When I said "Paulette Soucy , my voice was calm and clear.
I didn't sound at all like the screamy-meamy I had been
inside all morning. "I have the eleven o'clock interview," I
added. I sounded like a serious professional woman, not like
the exhausted waitress who walked around the Early Bird Cafe
filling cups of coffee for mill workers who were dressed in
yesterday's tired clothes. I sometimes wondered if Richard and
I would end up like them.

There was a large rubber tree plant next to my chair and
instinctively I passed my finger over it as I thought of all
the things I might have been doing at home. It was
overwhelming. Washing piles of laundry and Georgie's sheets
every time he pee-ed. (And when it was too cold to hang the
wash outside, we draped things all over the house.) Folding
clothes and doing the dishes all the time. Gardening, canning,
drying. It never seemed to end. And the next morning, there
was always the Early Bird. Every week we sent applications
out, but few of them materialized into interviews. There were
too many people like us vying for a category of public jobs
that had been dried up. With other people in government, it
could all have been different, and I sometimes felt bitter
about it.

Sitting in the lovely office, I began to fantasize being able
to turn the oil heat up sometimes instead of having to go
with Richard into the woods to cut blown-down trees. I was
thinking about this when a woman in a worsted suit, her hair
cut after a fashion portrayed on the cover of the magazine on
the end table right next to me, smiled as she walked by. I
could smell her perfume, it was a wild flower scent, and then
she entered a room where there were a number of voices.
They were women's voices, and I knew that was in my favor.

My own skirt was an expensive piece. Not that I had
bought it! A friend's sister had done that, and for a moment I
felt a violent anger at this woman who lived a long way away,
whom I had met only once. It was people like this friend's
sister and her husband, like the people in government now,
who were reshaping -- or perhaps their kind had always

shaped -- the world that people like Richard and I had to live in.

But that sort of thinking, I knew, would only spoil the coming interview. I knew I spoke well and quickly on my feet. And that's what I tried to focus on as I sat waiting. I felt strong and confident. Why shouldn't they hire me? I thought. I'm damn good, but I knew it had nothing to do with being "damn good". In the end, wouldn't it have to do with something else, something I could only fake?

There were seven of them when I walked in, seven demure, coiffed ladies, a few no older than I. They sat around an oblong table, smiling amiably as if we were about to have a social occasion. Around the room, there were large potted plants and the walls were covered with poster art.

When I saw that they were, as I had guessed, all women, my heart jumped for joy. A portion of my competition had probably been eliminated! Women like these who met in the morning were not women who worked away from home and I sensed they might not be confident about wielding authority over a man in the director's position. In fact, the last director had been a woman. The woman in the worsted suit, whose name was Mrs. George Allen, began the interview by reviewing my résumé. It was a good résumé, but it had gaps when I had decided to travel out west to experience living in the Rockies, when I had taken time to try to write a novel that had come to nothing. Then there were the jobs like waitressing that had not, of course, been written up. But, I was a woman. I could always say I was taking care of my children during these gaps. I would not seem shiftless and unreliable in a way that Richard who had, if anything, fewer gaps would. Only men who could not hold a real job and who were not real men stayed home to take care of their children!

"So what attracted you to this particular job?" said Mrs. Allen. When she said that, about being attracted to this job, I smiled a broad smile, but inside I could feel the acid of anger. What had attracted me was that it was only one of two in that particular week's want ads that had been suitable

for my skills. The times did not favor people like me. We had
had choosiness beaten out of us.

I heard myself re-enumerate my qualifications, summing
them up by saying, "And so, it seemed a challenging situation
for my background and interests."

Certainly more challenging and lucrative than waitressing at
a restaurant in the village! God, how I hated waitressing, but
it had turned out to be easier than being a clerk in a
clothing store. I had tried that too.

The women and I talked, and it was all so civilized, so
clean and unhurried. Nobody jumped up to grab a baby,
nobody begged off to go do some weeding or to split some
wood.

"We women have volunteered too long," said Mrs. George
Allen who was president of the board of the arts council. She
paused as if in thought and as she did so she reached deep
into her coiffure, with a long red-tipped finger to scratch
her scalp. "It's important for a woman who feels the need to
work beyond the home to receive the validation she's looking
for, to be compensated sufficiently to attain that validation."

Then she mentioned the salary; my heart leapt for joy.
New boots for the kids, a new, second-hand car, storm
windows instead of plastic for the house, more credential-
ization for Richard. And a movie and a drink out every once
in a while. How luxurious could life be!

"That would be fine," I said as if offers had come pouring
in on me and I would deign to accept this offer as worthy of
the ego of a woman of my position.

"And so we'll let you know how we decide," said Mrs.
Allen, whose husband it turned out was president of one of
the local banks. I left quickly. Fear flapped wildly. I was cold
and icy. Outside, clouds had suddenly had hidden the sky and
I darted across the parking lot that a row of rose bushes
separated from the street and made completely vulnerable to
the building.

When I had left, the women had taken a break, and I knew
they were able to see me down below anytime they chose to

stand at one of their second floor windows.

"Things will work out, somehow," I told myself as I got into the car. "Things will work out somehow."

Hastily I turned the key, just wanting to get away, to be safe at home. I needed to get far away from these women who did not know what kind of life I led.

When I turned the key, there was only a whine. I felt like a stone dropping into a well. I could feel the waters parting and then swallowing me up. I gagged for breath.

I turned the key again, hoping that I had somehow not done it right. All I heard was another whine, nothing more.

They would hear my old car whining, and they would look down to see who was trespassing in their parking lot. They would see me down here with my jumper cables, and Mrs. Allen and the others would realize I was not a woman like them.

O, Canada!

In summer, the sliding windows were kept open, and people walked by all day and all evening. If there was a breeze, it blew in. But now, the condensation on the windows blocked the view, and the room was stuffy with the smell of wool and of too many people.

David fingered the ashtray. A dream had awakened him in the night and since then, all day, he had been sure about his decision. He had struggled with what he should do for weeks, and now he was sure. But even so some part of him was holding out and he could feel the knots in his stomach.

Célestine said in a mockingly stern voice, "If you don't leave that ashtray alone, I'll flick my cigarette ashes on your hand." And then she did just that: she flicked ashes from her Gauloise so that they fell on his hand, but he did not move his hand. His eyes were on a spot directly in front of him on the table, and he had not seemed to notice what she had done.

She touched his hand. Startled, he looked up, and their eyes met.

"I'm sorry," she said.

His brows formed into a question.

"For the ashes, interfering in your reverie."

"Oh, it's nothing," he said, waving his hand away in a

gesture of dismissal.

"You'll come to visit, won't you?" she asked. "Perhaps you'll have a dream that will tell you to visit your poor Célestine. She'll be struggling through an intemperate Canadian winter, and she'll need all her dear friends."

"Yes, of course."

They might have been lovers, he thought. If they had married, he could have stayed because then he would be the spouse of a Canadian, but it had not worked that way.

She adjusted the scarf around her neck. "Without you here it'll be harder to get through this last month of winter. *Maudit hiver!* Tell me this is the last month."

"I hope so," he said. "It'll be in a small town where I'll be."

"Will you have to speak English all the time?"

"Most of the time."

"For me, that would be the hardest."

"I'm just different," he said. "What I want for myself. That'll be the hardest."

Beyond Célestine who tilted her head slightly to one side as she looked at him, he saw a table by the bar full of people speaking loudly. They were French. In Montréal, you could always pick out the French from the Québecois.

To the left, between David's table and the windows, there were two women and a man. The man and the tall, slender woman got up, and she put a thick wool hat on. She spread it apart with the backs of her hands and slid the hat down over her ears. Then, the two buttoned up, and the man reached to the floor next to the chair where he had been sitting and picked up his gloves. They looked at David and Célestine and smiled. The other woman who had remained seated kept looking at her coat. The man said something to her.

David was thinking about tomorrow. Tomorrow at this time, his bus would drive through the mill district, and he would get off at the downtown station. His parents would be there, and his father would say, "How long are you here for?"

David would shrug his shoulders and reply, "For a while." They would speak in French, and his mother would point out

that he spoke like a Québecois. He would be happy she had
said that; he might even want to say, "Yes, I have chosen to
become a Québecois."

Tomorrow evening, his father would say too, "What are you
going to do?" David wouldn't know then any more than he
knew now as he sat once again fingering the ashtray with
Célestine next to him talking to the three people from the
other table.

There are other kinds of people who would have assessed
right away the life available to him in Montréal. They would
not have had to spend two years of poverty and of constant
trying to piece things together before they would have known
that it was too difficult.

He felt foolish now; he felt that he had done things wrong.

When his father would ask the next evening what David was
going to do, he would mean work and so his father would add,
"I might be able to get you in. Until you found something
else, you know." And, from the bus station, they would drive
to his parents' house which was down a side street. In the
summer, people there kept plastic deer on their lawns, but in
the winter there were no deer on the lawns. How long could
he stay there? And then what would he do?

Célestine, who had been speaking to the man and the two
women, said, "*O, mais non, non!*" and everyone laughed.

David looked up. He saw the man, tall and handsome, and
the woman, svelte in her long coat and thick hat tilted to
one side. They said, "*Au revoir!*" and then they walked
between the many tables and chairs toward the door. The
woman who had remained behind looked at her coat and then
at David and Célestine. After a pause, she came to their table
and sat at the edge of one of the empty chairs.

"And I had a dream in which they were doing it," the
woman said to Célestine. Her cheeks were very full and her
mouth almost looked lost in them. "In my dream, a male figure
said to me, 'You will be safe as long as you keep your
balance'. And then I was balancing plates and some Americans
were trying to knock them down."

"We won't let them," said Célestine. There was a ripple of mirth running through Célestine's voice so that David could tell that something had gone on between her and this woman. Célestine had this quality when you first met her that made you believe she understood exactly what you meant. It was a wonderful gift that he had greatly appreciated his first days in Montréal when he had tried to understand why he had come, what was this powerful thing that had brought him there. It had driven him as a wind drives a canoe down a lake, overpowers it and its occupant and pushes it here or there.

He asked,"Who?"

"*Les américains!*"

"*Les maudits américains!*" he said so that the woman smiled. He thought , She is a girl, but he liked her, liked her smile. It pleased him that she was wondering if Célestine and he were lovers. Perhaps then, had they been, he thought again, they could have married and he would not be leaving.

Pointing to David, Célestine said to the woman, "An American devil himself speaking!"

The woman looked at David, then she looked at Célestine. "Come on!" she said.

He thought, This woman has deep emotions. Then, he said, shaking his head, "She tells that to everyone."

The woman had round cheeks and, when she smiled, they filled up with goodwill. He liked teasing this woman. "Anyone can see that I'm Québecois."

"You phoney!" shouted Célestine. "He's a half-breed. A Franco-American. He likes to pass for a real Québecois, but I always call his bluff."

"Ah, well. A Franco-American! That's not the same thing. For a moment, I thought you were going to say he was English. My name's Rose. What're yours?"

"Célestine."

"I'm David. You aren't Rrose Sélavy, are you?"

"No, I'm Rose Malo."

He felt embarrassed. It had come out like an exhalation of

breath, this literary allusion that no one but him would know.
And now he could see that she had shrivelled like a flower
placed too close to the radiator. Célestine, who was used to
him, laughed. "He's always making allusions to something or
other. I miss them most of the time."

"Oh," said Rose. "I'm sure I would miss them all the time.
Well, I'll go back to my table now. Nice meeting you."

She got up and waited.

Célestine said, "Sit down. Stay with us."

"But I must be interrupting something."

"Please join us," David said, feeling sorry about saying
Rrose Sélavy. He liked her in some way.

Rose bought them beers. He looked at her, and she smiled.
She said, "What do you do?"

Célestine was a student at *l'université de Québec*. David said
he was a writer.

Her eyes looked down and to the right and the weight of
her face fell so that she looked drawn and exhausted, and he
wondered what it was they had said that had made her sad.
She said, "Oh, I'm only an assembly line worker -- for an
American company." She pressed buttons on sweaters, and she
showed them what she did, using her sweater, taking the
fabric in one hand and pretending she had a button machine
in the other. "Boom, boom! I can do a couple of hundred a
day." She looked at them. They smiled. He reached for her
arm and stroked her. She gave him a wan smile and then said,
"But that's not what I want to do with my life."

"What do you want to do?" asked Célestine.

"I want to go to the university," she answered Célestine as
she looked at David. "I want to make something of myself."

Her face was quite round and her fingers looked like
sausage links--two longer links and one short one to each
finger. As a writer, he liked the image, but it had nothing to
do with the way he felt about her. He liked her.

By the bar, the large table full of French people began to
sing. At first, the song was just noise; then quickly the tune
and the words of the *Marseillaise* became clear.

"Goddamn French!" a man shouted. "Get the hell back to France." People laughed.

"Go colonize some other country," someone else bellowed, but the French sang even more loudly.

Rose said, "I don't understand them. Why they come here and do that. Why do they think we like it?"

From someplace by the entrance, a strong male voice intoned, *O, Canada!* There were perhaps a couple of hundred Québecois in the bistro and, as if on cue, they all rose to their feet. David stood with them. As he sang with the others, he paid no attention to the clichés, the maudlin tone, that had been used to eulogize their North American experience, their defense of a language and a people. It had been their anthem before the English had usurped it, and they sang it with pride because it was theirs.

The critic in him receded, and there were present before him only the singing and the bonds of history and language.

When at last they had finished, the Québecois broke into cheers and the table of Frenchmen, subdued, shouted, "*Bravo!*" Everyone sat down, and when he looked around he saw that there was a smile running through the room.

Célestine said, "We shouldn't have depended on the French in 1760!" And from a table next to theirs, a man leaned towards Célestine and said, "To hell with them!"

"Yes," she said. "Who needs them anyway! We've taken care of ourselves for the last two hundred years. We don't need anybody but ourselves."

"*Bravo,*" he said. "*Vive le Québec libre.*"

David was looking at his mug of beer. Rose said, "They taught you to sing *O, Canada!* that way in Maine?"

"Sometimes we sang it in town for occasions, sometimes at school."

"I don't even know all the words."

David shrugged his shoulders. "That kind of stuff comes easily to me," he said.

"I like singing it," she said. She sipped her beer. They were all quiet. "What do you write?"

"I freelance articles on Canadian topics for newspapers and magazines. I write from the francophone perspective. I write fiction too."

"I always wanted to be a writer," she said, looking down, her voice dropping. "I don't seem to be visited much by inspiration. Is that what you call it, inspiration?"

"Some people call it that. I don't know what I call it."

"Will you ever write about tonight, this?"

"Perhaps," he said, noticing that Célestine was looking around the room. Her eyes stopped on a table of men. There was a handsome man there, with a thick black beard. "It's just that what I write about comes from inside. I can't say for sure I'll ever write a story about this or that -- not like I could say I'd write an article."

"One teacher I had in school," Rose said, "thought it was like something that lived inside a person -- he called it an inner god. I had forgotten about that."

"Like going to communion and having little Jesus living inside for a while," said Célestine, but neither David nor Rose laughed.

"Yes, it's something like an inner god," said David, looking at Rose. He wanted very much to tell her how this struggle was going on inside at that very moment and how it would go on even when he was elsewhere. He wanted to tell her that tomorrow evening he would be arriving at the mill district on the bus and his parents would be there to drive him to their house on a side street where, in summer, people kept plastic deer on their lawns. His father would ask him what he was going to do. He would have to do something.

"His inner god has not volunteered to pay the rent," said Célestine.

"He's not a very responsible god. I guess you don't have to be when you're living in the ages. I'm tired of the hustle I've had to put up with. Some part of me has been very happy here, but many things need to be easier for me. It's like a child, and my David is its father. We're working out our relationship. It's not easy."

Rose smiled. "Who won today? Is it all in your writing?"

"I wrote nothing," he said, shrugging his shoulders.

"What! You let the pouting god win?"

He liked her playfulness.

"He's in between writings," said Célestine, adjusting her scarf. "He's going back tomorrow."

"Oh!" said Rose, looking at David. "Going back? Do you mean he's leaving Québec?" There was pain in her voice.

"Yes."

"David, I'm so sorry about what I said. I didn't think. It was so foolish. I just couldn't imagine your leaving!"

"Don't worry," said David, looking into his glass. "It's a good decision. I need to balance things. I'm mostly reconciled. I'm not selling enough articles to live on. I need a more substantial, regular income -- but I'm not a landed immigrant and so I can't get regular employment. I feel that I'm too poor and that is driving me more compellingly than that thing you call the 'inner god'."

"They wouldn't let you in?"

"No. I came anyway. I had once thought that being here would be enough. I bet everything on that."

"*Mon vieux,*" said Célestine. She spoke from someplace outside the intimacy he and Rose had had, like a person standing outside on the porch speaking through an open window. "I'll come to visit you. It won't be all that bad in Yankeeland." She patted his hand. "You write me a letter telling me how you're adapting, and I'll answer."

He would write long letters because he would need to prolong his experience, and she would send back a note saying she intended to write at length soon, but she would never do it. He would not be angry because he knew he would be writing the letters for himself.

"I have to go," said Célestine.

"Oh, me too," said Rose regretfully. "I wish we had met earlier. I mean, sooner than this evening."

"Yes," he said. He thought, She would have answered my letters. Rose and Célestine got up. "Don't stay to drink by yourself," said Célestine. "Go home and get a good night's sleep." She slipped into her coat.

"No, no, I won't stay," he said.

Rose looked at the windows, opaque with condensation. "I suppose it's still just as cold."

"One more month. I don't know how I'll make it," said Célestine, adjusting the scarf around her neck.

He got up. All around him people spoke French. He heard himself thinking, Why do I have to go? as Rose and Célestine exchanged addresses. Rose lives up my way, he thought, and then he remembered he was leaving. It had already stopped being 'his way'. Tomorrow, he would cross the Jacques-Cartier Bridge. If he turned his head then, he would see the mountain rise high and cold above the city and he would want to stay. He would hear a voice inside shouting desperately, "No, no!" But, it was impossible. He could not continue. "It's foolish, isn't it," said Rose. "All of these regulations! You have centuries of Québec in you crying for a now, for a life in the present."

Outside, the cold bit their cheeks and, before they arrived at Célestine's, near the massive, stone *cinémathèque québecoise,* David felt how his nostril hairs had gone stiff as he breathed in and out. Célestine said goodbye to them both and hugged them, and she said to David, "Don't forget Québec".

He said, "*Je me souviendrai.*"

"He will remember," said Rose, repeating David's words as she looked at him. "He will never forget even if he never comes back."

Célestine rushed up her stairs and entered her building. He thought of when he had first come to Montréal and he had been here at her apartment. They had had yogurt from little plastic containers and he had asked her if he could have them for drinking glasses and she had given him the containers along with three glasses from her cupboards. She had often been a good friend, he thought as he and Rose hurried through the cold, clutching their coats at the necks. Soon,

Rose stopped and said, "I go in here." There was a silence. It was bitterly cold. She reached up and kissed him. He could feel his cheek moist from her lips.

"I'm sorry you have to go."

She stood before him, hesitating, awkward, and he thought that if he were to say the least encouraging thing she would ask him to come inside with her.

"Thank you," he said. "I've enjoyed talking to you. This is a very difficult time for me. We might have been good friends."

Brusquely, awkwardly, like a racoon or a woodchuck scrambling away, Rose turned and ran up her stairs. He stood on the sidewalk looking at her. His breath came out white in the night air. When she reached her door, she did not turn around.

This whole thing was rather embarrassing, he thought, having to go back with nothing and his father asking him what he was going to do. He would not stay long there. He would go on to some other place, some US city, someplace where he had lived before and where he could get things together fast enough.

But he would always remember that moment, their all standing up like that, their being Québecois. His inner god, as Rose had called it, liked that kind of show. What a joke, David thought, this inner god not needing to worry about the next meal, concerned only with the sweep of history and the making of art!

Looking at the city around him, he said, "*O, mon beau Canada!*" and softly he began to sing the song to himself. He knew all the words.

Looking Back

What the hell did you know at twenty-two, Gene thought, really know about life and about what might be going to follow you around for the rest of it, like a shadow, making things dark wherever you went? Because you couldn't see it just then, you were young and the sun was in your face, how could you know about a darkness, behind you, about to follow you, into your old age?

Gene was frightened, at twenty-two, but he didn't know he was frightened, frightened of being the only one left, alone, without anyone to kick around with. It seemed to him at twenty-two that a man of twenty-two should be ready to live a man's life and, if he were not, then being ready might come with doing the things men did who were ready.

His father had, after all, gotten married at twenty-two. But Gene still had guys to kick around with. He was not away yet, not lonely in a barrack, barren and ugly, not thinking of Sunday meals and of visiting his father's parents with the whole family and everywhere people speaking the French that warmed him like the comforter on his bed at home on a cold night. He wanted to be part of that, but he did not know what it would mean, what it would cost in dreams. How could you, at twenty-two, he thought now, how could you have known?

He had grown lonely, away. He had missed his mother and father. He had thought, as if he were setting things up for himself, that he would marry Muriel. It had seemed a good idea to be a man, to be what a man was, to do everyday, every year, what a man did, to "work towards something". He was tired of being unsure. He wanted to be sure, to be happy.

"Oh, Eugène," she said when he finally reached her over the phone -- a big deal in those days. He had had to have an operator make an appointment with Muriel. How impatiently, Muriel said later, she had waited for two o'clock to roll around to hear what she wanted to hear.

"Oh Gene, yes, yes." And shouldn't they be married on his very next furlough, and oh yes August was so pretty, and oh three days isn't very long but if it's all he had, and don't say that -- a lot of men return from overseas ok, on their feet, but you're right just the same. We shouldn't put anything off.

Their day in August, the day that was to make him a man, that day had been hot and steamy and he had stood, nervous, apprehensive, and hopefully handsome, in his uniform and had felt the perspiration trickle down his side. Even now, sitting in the kitchen, watching TV and thinking of all of this, he could remember having been hot and uncomfortable and having thought: I'm married. At last, I'm a man.

He was happy then because he had done something he had thought about all his life and he had wondered what it would be like and he had known that being married was not the same as making love and he had thought about that all his life too and had wondered what that would be like and that night they would do it and perhaps they'd have a baby and if something happened to him there would be a child to follow.

In those days when they were young and there was no way to know that they would not have everything they wanted, they had said to each other that the children, whoever they would be, would finish high school. High school was special. It was called the best years of your life, but it had not been for them.

Muriel and he had left school, school which was home to *les américains* but not to them, for what seemed good reasons then, at the time, but seemed like less good reasons to their children who did not understand what it was like to be laughed at by the Yankee teachers when you said "I like that, me", said it just like you breathed the air.

After quitting school, he had gone to Connecticut with his cousin Jacques. There he worked in a White Tower Restaurant, washing dishes, and then he apprenticed at Pratt-Whitney. His father had said proudly to everyone that Eugène had a good job.

Later Gene moved to the shipyards in New Jersey where the money was very good just before the war. You could earn $2.00 an hour. Gene's father had worked all his life and was not earning $2.00 an hour. It didn't seem to Gene in New Jersey that a high school diploma was going to make any difference to a person who was doing as well as he was.

Then one morning, he sat listening to the morning radio, savoring a cigarette before heading for Mass with his roommate, his cousin Jacques, and it shot through him like a torpedo: Pearl Harbor. He and Jacques talked about it and they enlisted. They were young and could do anything. And Muriel was always there. Not quite his sweetheart but someone special back home.

Later, it seemed like a radio drama, that period when he bought a diamond and called her up to ask her to marry him and then they had gotten married one weekend. Afterwards she had come with him and worked in a munitions factory not far from the base. It didn't take long before he was shipped overseas and she had stayed to work and had put away money to buy their first house. Selling it years later hadn't brought back to them all they had invested. There were three children by that time.

Muriel spent all those years alone before they were married and afterwards, later, when he was gone so much, working at night after his regular job, working on Saturdays. Muriel worked between pregnancies and quit when the children cried every day and the lady next door who babysat locked them out all morning and all afternoon. He had said Muriel was to stay home: a mother should be with her children: they would manage somehow without her working. She gave "parties" and they got plastic dishes and clothes and housecleaning detergents cheaper than at the store.

When they finally emerged from the house parties and the sixty-hour weeks, from this mean life he hadn't known he'd have when he set off to make big money in Connecticut before the war, he had no more hair on top of his head; his temples were salted with white; his children were grown-up and the whole world had changed.

It was so long ago; he really couldn't remember what he had known then about the time that was to become now. Had he really thought that Muriel would not want the farm that he had dreamed of? Could he have known that they would not feel the same way about furniture and home and clothes for the kids? Feel together so that they would hum like a new motor in fine tune and not clang and bang so that things would wear down between them?

They had had the children, five in all, strewn across the years of their youth, so that, when it was all over, when they finally emerged, they were very tired and he no longer felt like beginning. He had simply thought that that was the way things were. Working nights, when he was tired, working Saturdays, when he was thinking of the garden, its soil dark and friable now, waiting for him. What else could he have done during those years when they needed to buy shoes and dental care and flour? He was a man like his father and he did things a man did. It was easy in those days to know, as he did not know now, what a man did. Later, it was not so easy because people like his children did things he did not understand.

His children spoke like other people's children, certainly not like his own. They had gotten loans and scholarships and college diplomas. They had become like houses that are extensively remodeled, houses that you can't recognize anymore.

His own life seemed like a ranch house that had been built without the right plans, the plans he had provided, once.

What if? he thought. What if I had bought the farm I wanted back in '47 instead of the house Muriel preferred? What if I had stayed in the service as a career man or what if I had finished the apprenticeship at Pratt-Whitney instead of going for the higher paying job in New Jersey?

Ah! but there was no way to know!

SOLEIL PRESS

For additional copies of *What Became of Them and Other Stories From Franco-America,* please send $8.95 for each book along with $1.50 handling for up to three books and $.75 for each additonal book thereafter.

*

SOLEIL PRESS is preparing an anthology of contemporary Franco-American writings. If you are interested in being notified of its publication, please send your name and address.

SOLEIL PRESS
RFD#1, Box 452
Lisbon Falls, Maine 04252